JF
HILDICK

Hildick, E. W.
The case of the
fantastic
footprints

THE CASE OF THE
FANTASTIC FOOTPRINTS

By the Same Author

The Case of the Fantastic Footprints

A McGurk Mystery

BY E. W. HILDICK

Macmillan Publishing Company   New York

Maxwell Macmillan Canada   Toronto

Maxwell Macmillan International
New York   Oxford   Singapore   Sydney

Macmillan Publishing Company is part of the Maxwell Communication
Group of Companies.

Macmillan Publishing Company
866 Third Avenue, New York, NY 10022

Maxwell Macmillan Canada, Inc.
1200 Eglinton Avenue East, Suite 200
Don Mills, Ontario M3C 3N1

First edition
Printed in the United States of America

10 9 8 7 6 5 4 3 2 1
The text of this book is set in 12 point Caledonia.
Library of Congress Cataloging-in-Publication Data
Hildick, E. W. (Edmund Wallace), date.
    The case of the fantastic footprints : a McGurk mystery / by E.W.
  Hildick.—1st ed.
        p.   cm.
Summary: McGurk and his team of detectives investigate the strange footprints that
have begun to appear in wet cement all over their neighborhood.
    ISBN 0-02-743967-4
  [1. Mystery and detective stories.]   I. Title.
  PZ7.H5463Casdc   1994[Fic]—dc20   93-28735

Contents

THE CASE OF THE
FANTASTIC FOOTPRINTS

1 Wrongfully Accused

"Hey, McGurk! We need your help!"

We stared as Ray Williams burst into our HQ that Friday afternoon.

Willie Sandowsky looked startled. He'd had his back to the door.

But Brains Bellingham, Mari Yoshimura, Wanda Grieg, and I looked hopeful.

We'd been sitting at the battered round table in McGurk's basement, arguing about how to spend the weekend. It looked like it would be the third in a row without a case for us to tackle.

McGurk stopped rocking in his chair and glared. He's got a good face for glaring, with his fiery red hair and the freckles that bunch up like thunderclouds. "This is a private meeting!" he rumbled.

Ray scowled right back. He's got a good *scowling* face. Thin. Hungry-looking. Furthermore, he's thirteen, a whole year older than any of us, and he acts like he knows it. "Yeah!" he growled. "A private meeting of the McGurk Organization. Private *detectives*, right?"

"Sure," said McGurk. "So?"

"I just told you," said Ray. "We need your help."

" 'We'?" murmured McGurk, signaling to me, the Organization's record keeper, to open my notebook.

"Yeah!" said Ray. "Whiskers and me."

"Oh, dear!" said Wanda. "Whiskers isn't missing again, is he?"

Before Ray could reply, McGurk said, "If he is, you can forget it. We're not in the business of tracing stray cats."

"Huh!" Ray grunted. "I remember you said that last time, McGurk. And look what happened. When you *did* do the right thing, it put you in the way of busting a gang of interstate cat thieves. . . . But okay. If you don't want to take our case—"

"I didn't say that," said McGurk. "If there's a real problem, let's hear it. You said 'case.' Like it was a genuine, cut-and-dried, concrete case."

For the first time, a smile hovered on Ray's lips. Or it could have been a snarl. "Oh, it's *concrete* all right!"

"Well, go on," I said. "Exactly what *is* the case?"

"Being unjustly accused of doing criminal damage," said Ray.

"Damage to what?" asked McGurk.

"A driveway," said Ray.

McGurk stopped in midrock. "How can a *cat* do criminal damage to a *driveway*?"

"By walking on it when—" Ray began.

"Aw, come on!" McGurk jeered. "April Fools' Day was *weeks* ago!"

Ray's scowl deepened. "By walking on it before the concrete's set, dummy! *That's* how. They say it's his paw marks."

McGurk took a deep breath. This was different. "Who says it was Whiskers?"

"Sandra Ennis, for one," said Ray.

"Oh, *her!*" said Wanda, giving her long yellow hair a contemptuous toss.

"Quiet, Officer Grieg!" said McGurk. "Did she actually see Whiskers doing it? And does she have backup witnesses?"

"No," said Ray. "How could she, when he didn't do it? All she says is that she saw him snooping around the day before."

"Whose driveway was this?" I asked.

"Old Ms. Ennis's. Sandra's aunt Jane. Next door to her."

"So what?" said Wanda. "Cats do go straying onto wet concrete. And dogs. Kids, too. Why"—her face softened—"my own footprints are set on our patio. I was only three, and Mom says she wouldn't have them removed for the world, they're so cute."

"Yes, well," said Ray, "Ms. Ennis doesn't look at it like that. Whiskers isn't *her* cat."

"Well, *tough!*" said Wanda. "Cats can't be held legally responsible for something like that."

"But I keep telling you it wasn't Whiskers *anyway!*" said Ray. "I've examined his paws. Thoroughly. Through a magnifying glass."

"And?" said McGurk.

"And there wasn't a trace; not a speck of dried cement anywhere on them."

"But Sandra Ennis says she saw him hanging around, huh?" McGurk murmured.

"Yeah," said Ray. "And on the strength of *that*, Ms. Ennis has already called my dad, complaining."

McGurk sighed. Obviously, he still wasn't all that thrilled. But any old case was welcome just then.

"Okay," he said. "We'll take your assignment. If Whiskers didn't do it, we'll prove it."

"Yes, but how, Chief McGurk?" asked Mari.

"By taking accurate scientific measurements," he said. "Officer Bellingham, is your Polaroid camera in working order?"

"Sure," said our science expert, his short hair seeming to bristle more than ever.

"So go get it," said McGurk. "And bring some of your fancy measuring instruments. Then we'll visit the scene of the—uh—*alleged* crime."

Brains was already out the door.

"Meanwhile," McGurk continued, "you go bring along

the accused, Ray. So we can measure his paws and clear his name right away."

Ten minutes later, we all set out. Brains now had with him what he calls his forensic bag (an old black briefcase of his father's), while Ray was clutching a zippered airline bag in which the accused was protesting noisily.

"Hey!" a voice called out before we'd hit the street. "Where do you think you're going?"

It was Mrs. McGurk.

"A case, Mom."

"You said you were going to make a start on fixing that sandpile corner. Ready for when your cousin Dwayne comes."

"But that won't be until Memorial Day! Weeks away!"

"Yes. But I know you, Jack McGurk. Soon it'll be *days* away. Then *hours* away. Then *minutes* away. . . ."

McGurk was looking desperate. "Mom, I promise you. This won't take long. Then I'll get straight onto it."

"Sure!" grumbled Mrs. McGurk, as we all trooped off.

2 The Silent Sentinel

At first it was fairly quiet outside Ms. Ennis's house.

And we didn't have to look far for the prints. They were right at the end of the driveway, crisscrossing it.

"Beautiful!" murmured Brains. "Clear and firm!"

"Are these the actual prints?" McGurk asked Ray.

"Yeah."

They certainly *looked* like cat prints—the track of an animal that had seen something strange about the driveway's surface and couldn't resist investigating it.

McGurk had me make a diagram of this, and here it is:

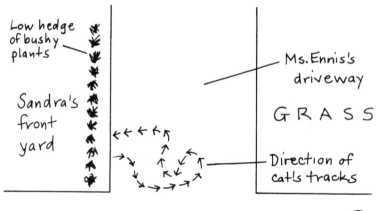

"They're cat prints all right," said Ray. "But not Whiskers's."

They'd set solid. To get them out, that part of the driveway would have to be completely resurfaced. I began to see why Ms. Ennis was so miffed.

Farther up, nearer the garage, another stretch seemed to have been more recently repaired. It had been roped off. There was a notice hanging from the rope. I made a sketch of this, too, and here's a copy:

Ms. Ennis's gleaming white Mercedes had had to be parked out on the street.

"Okay, Officer Bellingham," said McGurk. "Here's an extra-clear specimen."

He was pointing to one of the prints nearest the sidewalk. Brains was already fixing a flash bar to his camera.

By now, a small crowd of kids was beginning to gather.

"Stand back!" said McGurk. "Can't you see an investigation is in progress?"

"Investigation!" jeered a familiar voice.

It was Sandra Ennis. She was standing at the other

side of the line of bushy plants. Normally, when she widens those blue eyes, she can look the picture of innocence. But there was a rather nasty sneering gleam in them now.

"I suppose you're trying to prove that that Whiskers thing didn't make those paw marks, huh?"

"Whiskers is not a *thing*!" growled Ray.

"Oh, just tell her to get lost," said Wanda.

"No one tells *me* to get lost!" snapped Sandra. "Not when I'm on my parents' property. Or"—she took a step over the plants—"or on my aunt Jane's property. *You* get lost!"

"*We* are on *public* property," said Wanda, planting her feet firmly apart on the sidewalk. "You just try and—"

"That's enough, Officer Grieg!" said McGurk. He turned to Sandra. "Our client tells us you didn't actually see his cat walk on the wet concrete."

"No, but he was near it," she said. "And I didn't see any *other* cat around."

"That's just circumstantial evidence," said McGurk.

"Circumstantial, schmircumstantial!" sneered Sandra. "This is an open-and-shut case. It—hey! What's *he* doing?"

Our science expert was carefully pouring some white liquid out of a small bottle onto the selected paw mark.

"It's okay," he said, straightening up. "It's only a drop

of half-and-half to show up the pattern when I take my picture. It'll wipe off easily enough."

He stooped again, camera at the ready, his finger on the button.

Then came the flash, and everybody gasped.

But not because of the flash.

Oh, no. . . .

It was the sudden swift movement—a blur of chocolate and fawn—that hurtled itself toward Brains, and his howl as that blur landed plumb on his back and settled there in the shape of a Siamese cat.

Sandra laughed. "Serves you right! And keep still, or she'll dig her claws in deeper!"

"Get it *off* of me!" howled Brains, still bent double.

"I'm coming," said Sandra, taking her time.

"Hurry up, then!" wailed Brains. *"Please!"*

"Officer Rockaway," said McGurk, as Sandra picked up the cat, *"you* take charge of the camera until Officer Bellingham pulls himself together."

As it nestled in Sandra's arms, the Siamese squeezed its eyes, looking as if it had done something very clever.

"It seems like it's *your* cat," McGurk said.

"Yes," she said. "We got her a week ago. Tweelak. A purebred Siamese."

"That is why she jumped on Brains's back, Chief McGurk," said Mari. "We had one once that kept doing that. It is in their genes."

"You bet!" said Sandra. "They used to guard the ancient Siamese temples. If any prowlers came along, snooping and stooping, they jumped on their backs and dug in until the guards arrived. 'Silent sentinels,' they called them."

"Well, this isn't an ancient temple!" Brains protested, with his shirt pulled up around his neck while Willie examined his back.

I thought I could see some specks of blood, but just then I was more interested in the Polaroid shot.

"Hey!" I said. "This has come out beautifully, Brains. Congratulations!"

It was more than just a clear picture obtained under very difficult circumstances. Just take a look:

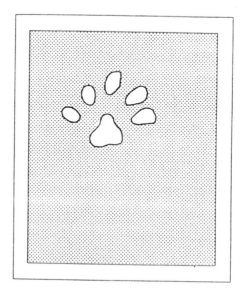

That one photo was enough.

I heard Wanda gasp. She was looking over my shoulder, while McGurk was putting some very sharp questions to Sandra Ennis.

"You said you didn't see any other cat around except Whiskers," he said. "How do we know this—uh—Tealark didn't make the marks?"

"The name is *Tweelak*," Sandra said. "And we know *she* didn't go walking over wet concrete. She is too intelligent, too *fastidious* about stepping into gunk. Aren't you, baby?"

While Tweelak was squawking her reply, Wanda had been finding *her* voice.

"Why, *that*," she said, stabbing a finger at the picture, "and *those*," she added, stabbing at the prints themselves, "they're the marks of a six-toed cat! Ray"—she spun around—"how many toes does Whiskers have?"

Ray looked taken by surprise. "Huh? Five, of course. Whiskers is a regular cat. *He's* no freakish— Why? Why do you ask?"

"Hey, McGurk!" Wanda called out. "Just see what—"

But McGurk had overheard what she'd been saying. He held up his hand for Wanda to be silent, then turned to Sandra. "Would you mind holding out one of your cat's front paws?"

"You'll find no dried cement *there*," said Sandra, doing

as he'd requested. She spoke triumphantly. Obviously *she* hadn't heard Wanda's remarks.

"No, only my blood!" growled Brains.

"Be quiet, Officer Bellingham," murmured McGurk, getting as close as he dared to the outstretched paw. "Well, what d'you know, Officer Grieg? *This* is a six-toed cat!"

Sandra began to bluster. "But—but—"

"But nothing!" said McGurk. "We now have proof. Photographic evidence plus the actual prints. It was *your* cat who was the perpetrator!"

"But six-toed cats aren't all *that* uncommon!" said Sandra. "Why, I bet that mangy old cat *Whiskers* is a six-toed cat!"

"Show her, Ray," McGurk said softly.

"Sure thing!" said Ray.

And he unzipped the bag.

Well, Whiskers had been toted around in there for over half an hour, his protests ignored. And although it took him a few seconds to get his bearings—long enough for Ray to hold out one of his paws and prove he only had five toes—Whiskers's eyes suddenly fell on Tweelak.

It was as if he knew that she'd been the cause of all this discomfort and indignity.

With a howl of rage, he flew out of the bag, just as Tweelak flew out of Sandra's arms. The onlookers, who'd already raised a cheer when they realized Whiskers had been cleared, now cheered even louder as the indignant brown tabby chased the pedigree Siamese up the driveway and all along the wet, newly laid concrete.

"I guess we can't get Whiskers off this rap, McGurk," said Wanda.

Ms. Ennis had already emerged to see what the hullabaloo was all about.

"No, but this time the damage can soon be repaired," I said, noticing a guy with a baseball cap come around from the back of the house and immediately set to work smoothing out the fresh paw marks.

Sandra and Ray were now approaching Ms. Ennis, carrying their wriggling animals. Sandra looked very subdued as Ray held out one of Whiskers's paws and started talking.

"I guess we can leave it to Ray to tie up the loose ends," said McGurk. "Come on, men. We've done *our* job. And I've just had a brilliant new idea."

③ The FTL

McGurk wouldn't tell us what his great idea was until we were back in his basement. Then: "Right, men," he said. "What this organization needs is a—" He thought for a moment. Then his face brightened. "An FTL."

We stared.

"A *what*, McGurk?" I said.

"An FTL. A footprint-testing laboratory."

We looked at one another. Some rolled their eyes upward. Brains, however, had sat bolt upright, his eyes shining behind his big glasses.

"What kind of a laboratory is that, McGurk?" he said. "Exactly?"

McGurk began slowly rocking. "One that will give us special training facilities. Not just for *identifying* footprints—sizes and patterns and such. But one where we can practice *interpreting* footprints—figuring out what whoever made them was doing."

A stir of interest went around the table.

"I—I don't quite get it, McGurk," I said.

"Well," he said, "think. Take this latest case. Those tracks in Ms. Ennis's driveway. Even if the perpetrator didn't have six toes, they'd have given us a valuable clue to whose cat it was."

"Uh—how?" asked Brains.

"By showing which direction it came from and which direction it went."

"Which direction *did* the tracks go, Chief McGurk?" Mari asked.

"You'd know if you'd observed them closely, Officer Yoshimura. Like I did." McGurk swept us all with a fierce glance. "And like you *all* will, after a few sessions with the FTL. . . . They came from Sandra's yard, as it happens. And after wandering around on the concrete, that's where they returned."

Everyone was looking impressed.

"So let's get on with constructing it," he said, standing up.

"Yes," said Wanda. "Let's. Just exactly what do you have in mind, McGurk?"

"I'll show you. Follow me, men."

He led the way to a corner of his backyard. There was a golden heap of new sand there already, next to what looked like a weed-choked vegetable bed.

Suddenly the alarm bells began to ring in my head. I remembered that that oblong of earth had once contained sand for McGurk to play in when he was as little as his cousin Dwayne. Could this be another scheme for getting us to do his chores?

But before I could voice this, he'd started to explain. "What we are going to do, men, is clear this space and fill it with this fresh sand. And first—"

"Here we go again!" said Wanda. "Well, if you think we're—"

But McGurk was racing on. "We'll line the space with plastic sheeting, so the weeds won't start shooting up again. And we'll put some boards around the edges to make it look businesslike. Then we'll round it off by giving the new sand a fine flat surface that'll simulate wet concrete."

Wanda's protests had died in her throat.

"And *on* that simulated wet concrete," McGurk continued, looking around at the five pairs of now deeply interested eyes, "we can replicate all kinds of prints and study them carefully."

That did it. The jerk had hooked us yet again!

There was a rush for spades and shovels, hammers, nails, rakes, and the water sprinkler. And in less than half an hour, there it was—a golden oblong, about nine feet by six feet, with McGurk giving it the final wetting with the sprinkler.

"Now what?" said Brains, almost dancing with eagerness to get his little feet busy on that beautiful surface.

"First," said McGurk, "I want you all to step inside, in turn, me first. Leave your prints, just one set each, one officer's behind another's."

So we did, and this was the result, which I sketched in my notebook before drawing it more carefully later:

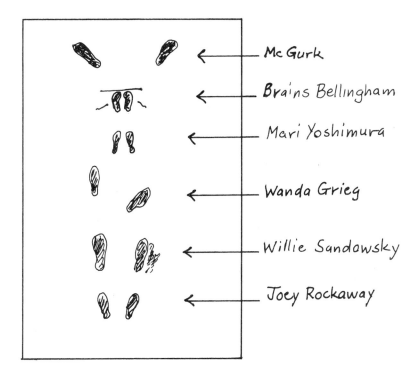

"Good!" said McGurk. "Excellent! Now I can explain just what I mean about interpretation. From these prints, we're able to tell something about the persons making them."

Well, I wasn't sure about *that!* But as he talked us through, I had to hand it to him. There *were* things to be learned from those marks in the sand.

"Like these," he said, pointing to his own. "Feet astride, ready for anything. The prints of a firm leader."

There was a murmur, but he was already bending to Brains's.

"Yes," he drawled slowly. "Interesting. A very, very precise kind of person. Look at the guideline he made." He turned. "Did you note that, Officer Rockaway?"

I nodded, but he peered closer at my notebook.

"What's with these whiskery lines at the sides? I don't see any in the sand."

"Well," I said, "those are his shoelaces. They didn't leave any marks visible to the naked eye, but they're undone, see. As they often are."

Sure enough, Brains was already bending to tie them up, blushing at my comment.

McGurk grunted. "Note only what you *see*, Officer Rockaway. Okay?"

He went on to Mari's. "A small person of course. Also very precise, but tidy with it. Modest, too—look at the way the toes turn in slightly. And *very* reliable."

Leaving Mari beaming in a not particularly modest way, he bent over Wanda's prints. "Now this set—"

"Yeah?" growled Wanda menacingly.

"The prints of a very feisty person," said McGurk. "Observe the fighting stance, men. Left foot forward. . . . Tends to jump to conclusions, though." (Another, softer growl from Wanda.) "But, like I say—feisty, up-front."

McGurk moved on. "Oh, boy!" he said, looking at Willie's prints. "The biggest person in the group, obviously. But kind of awkward, uncertain. See the way the right foot shuffled around before coming to rest." He clapped a hand on Willie's shoulder. "But that's okay, Officer Sandowsky. It's your sensitive nose that counts in this organization—not the way you move."

Willie cheered up. I thought for a second he was going to get down and shove his golden nose into the sand and leave *its* mark there.

But McGurk was now standing next to my prints. "Yes. *Another* well-balanced stance. Not exactly a leader's, but evenhanded—uh—even-*footed*. The marks of a good record keeper—when he doesn't let his imagination run away with him."

I was about to point out that it was all very well reading our characters from our footprints when he *knew* who'd made them, but what if we'd been complete strangers?

"It's all very well—" I began.

Then Ray Williams showed up, all smiles.

"I've come to thank you guys," he said. "We owe you

one. If your basement ever gets infested with rats, Whiskers will be only too pleased to come over and—"

"Fine," grunted McGurk. "Uh—how did it go with Ms. Ennis?"

Ray's grin widened. "A breeze! She isn't such a bad person, after all. She soon saw the point about the toes."

"How about Sandra and Tweelak?" asked Wanda.

"Well, *she* just had to take back her accusations, naturally. But she did keep on about how it must have been some *other* six-toed cat."

"How did her aunt take that?" asked McGurk.

"Well, she *might* have gone along with it," said Ray. "But the guy who'd been working on the driveway had been listening. And he said that now he'd come to think of it, he'd had to shoo Tweelak away from the driveway twice, the day before yesterday. She hadn't made any prints *then*, but she was obviously interested."

"And how did Sandra take *that*?" Wanda asked.

"She got nasty," said Ray. " 'Well, maybe it was some *other* Siamese,' she said. 'Or maybe you'd been drinking. Maybe you'd been *seeing* things.' Then she walked away, all hoity-toity."

Mari gasped. "What a rude thing to say to the man!"

"Anyway," said Ray, "the bottom line is Ms. Ennis was convinced it wasn't Whiskers and she went straight to the phone and apologized to my dad."

*　　*　　*

That made us all feel good. A nice neat end to the case, with justice done and seen to be done. But *as* a case I didn't think much of it. I mean, *none* of us had any idea that first afternoon how this was to develop into one of the most baffling and bizarre problems in the McGurk Organization's history. And, being so evenhanded and fair-minded, let me just add this: *Not even McGurk himself realized just what a useful tool his FTL was going to be in helping us to solve that mystery in the busy and mind-boggling weeks ahead.*

4 Footprints of a Monster?

All this took place during the last week of April and the first week of May.

It had been a hard winter, with a lot of frost damage. Not just to driveways, but also to garden paths, patios, and the edges of pools and ponds—places like that. And to public highways. A blacktop-resurfacing crew was steadily working its way along Pine Avenue. The special bitumen they were using didn't easily take marks of things as light as cats' paws or even human footprints. In fact, one of the men had started recommending bitumen for ordinary driveways. That was when he heard what was happening with the wet concrete and the dozens of new prints that had started to appear.

Naturally, the McGurk Organization soon focused on those prints.

At first, most of them turned out to be accidents. Other cats who'd gone snooping, like Tweelak, and two or three dogs. Then there were cases of little kids who hadn't looked where they were going. Most of these had been seen doing it, so no other cat or dog or kid got wrongly accused, the way Whiskers had.

Then there were the marks of kids who'd been *allowed* to leave their prints as mementos. Most of these Hall of Fame types were of one foot only, carefully pressed down to leave a clear mark. And, of course, there was no mystery about any of *them*.

But then examples of deliberate vandal acts started to crop up. Done by older kids or adults. And I do mean deliberate.

We could be pretty certain about this. McGurk had had us simulating genuine blunders at our FTL.

"Remember, this is supposed to be a patch of wet concrete, men," he'd announced. "I want you to approach it pretending to be thinking of something else. And before you know it, you've stepped onto the wet concrete."

Well, it was very useful. At the end we all had a much better idea of the kind of prints to look for when they'd been made accidentally.

McGurk had me make a chart of the results to pin up on the wall. Here's a copy:

FOOTPRINTS MADE BY ACCIDENT
AT THE McGURK ORGANIZATION FTL

Name of Officer	Sample Print(s)	Remarks
Grieg, W.	Edge of sand bed	Single print, made by quickly withdrawn foot before it made full impression. (Note: Lighter at front of foot.)
Sandowsky, W.	3. 4. 5. 1. 2. 6.	The prints of a real dreamer who goes on for several steps, then panics when he realizes what he's been walking on.
Bellingham, G.	Edge of sand bed	Print — or Half-print only, made by someone pulling up right at the edge.
Yoshimura, M.	Edge of sand bed	The print of a careful person who realizes his/her mistake immediately and tries to put it right by scraping wet cement back over it. (Note how footprint still shows faintly under the scrape lines.
Rockaway, J.	Edge of sand bed	Same as Officer Yoshimura's, only bigger and showing a longer stride. Also footprint showing more clearly because, being highly imaginative, I made allowance for wet cement being harder to scrape back than wet sand.

(You'll notice that there is no sample print for McGurk. And why? I quote: "Because I don't make false steps, men. *I* keep my eyes open at all times." The jerk.)

Anyway, this helped us spot the deliberate marks immediately. Like the prints of the person we were soon to be calling the Hopping Man. . . .

It wasn't until Tuesday afternoon that we got to hear about them. They'd been made the night before at the house next door to Ms. Ennis on East Birch. The lady came and told us about it in person.

"Are you Jack McGurk?" she said. "Head of the McGurk Corporation?"

"The McGurk *Organization*, ma'am," said McGurk. "Yes."

He was looking at her sharply. She's a plump, pleasant-looking woman who is usually smiling. She wasn't now, though. She looked nervous, shaken.

"Well, I'm Mrs. Jacobs," she said. "Jane Ennis recommended you. The police don't seem too interested, but Jane told me about how you'd solved *her* problem. With the cat prints."

"Cats again, ma'am? Did you notice how many toes—?"

"No, no!" said Mrs. Jacobs. "It's much more serious than cats. This looks like the work of a—a person. And a very strange person indeed. If you'll come with me, I'll show you."

We didn't need to be asked twice. And as we hurried to the scene, she began to explain.

"My husband isn't home yet. I only discovered it myself after he'd left for work. I noticed the plastic sheet had been moved. He'd covered it with plastic to protect it. I thought maybe it had been blown away by a gust of wind. But no. . . ."

McGurk was red in the face, trying to get a word in, dying to know what she was referring to—a patio, a driveway, or what.

By now, however, we were walking up the driveway itself, and it was only when we turned the corner that we saw what she'd been talking about.

No, not the patio. But *on* the patio.

A wooden framework, six feet by four feet, divided into six squares, each containing a slab of wet concrete. At least what had *been* wet concrete. Now it was dry and hard and looking like this:

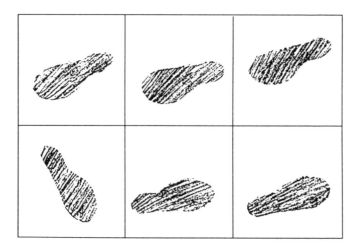

"My husband was making his own pavers," said Mrs. Jacobs. "Using his own molds. Saving the hassle and cost of transporting them here ready-made."

McGurk was bending over the deep massive footprints. "All produced by one foot, men," he murmured. "The left."

"Yes, Chief McGurk," Mari said. "It looks as if he hopped around those squares."

"Wow! Yeah!" said Willie. "Like a game of hopscotch!"

Wanda shivered. "Ugh! A grown man, too!"

"A *very big* grown man," Brains said in an awed voice. He was already on his knees, busy with his tape measure. "Thirteen and one-half inches long. That's some shoe size!"

Everyone fell silent.

I knew how they were all feeling. I, for one, got a mental picture of a huge, lumbering figure with the mind of a child, playing hopscotch on wet concrete in the middle of the night!

A kind of Frankenstein's Monster figure . . .

5 McGurk Takes a Tumble

"The sole and heel pattern is very clear," said Mari.

She was right. Each print showed up as clearly as the next. They reminded me of those left by kids with tolerant parents—apart from the size, of course.

In fact, another mental picture flashed into my head. The picture of Dr. Frankenstein standing in the shadows, saying to his monster, "That's right, son. Hop very carefully and make sure your footprints come out nice and clear. . . . *That's* my boy!"

Mrs. Jacobs nodded at Mari. "Yes, I'd say that pattern makes a very good clue."

McGurk grunted. He hates it when clients try to tell him his job.

"What are you doing, McGurk?" Wanda asked.

He was standing on his left leg, just getting ready to hop. Not *on* the squares, but at the side, level with each of the monster prints.

"Just checking the direction, Officer Grieg. Remember"—he started to hop—"it isn't . . . just the pattern . . . but the direction . . . that could give us . . . a clue."

Like that, with a new hop between each phrase.

Then he borrowed my notebook and made his own rough diagram. "Like this," he said.

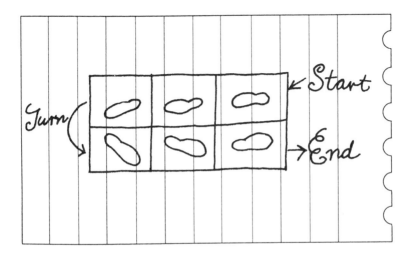

"*That* was the direction the perpetrator went, men. Counterclockwise."

"So what?" said Brains.

"I can't say for sure," McGurk admitted. "But it's always useful to put yourself in the perp's place. To—uh—follow in his footsteps. It *could* give you a hint about what was on his mind. To help with his profile."

At the word "profile" our science expert perked up.

But Mrs. Jacobs didn't seem impressed. "I'd say just doing as much malicious damage as possible is what was on his mind," she said. "Clockwise or counterclockwise."

"What if he hopped *backward*?" said Willie. "Then he'd a started where you ended."

"We're looking for a vandal, Willie," said Wanda. "Not a circus act!"

Mari was off on a different tack. "They say it is a sign of witchcraft, doing things counterclockwise. Casting evil spells."

"Oh, dear!" said Mrs. Jacobs.

"Piffle!" said Brains. "Unscientific garbage!"

"Not so fast, Officer Bellingham," said McGurk. "Any witches among your acquaintance, ma'am?"

Mrs. Jacobs shook her head, still looking uneasy. "None that I know of. And certainly no one who wears combat boots *that* size!"

"No, well, we have to look into all possibilities, ma'am." McGurk turned. "Officer Bellingham, go get your camera and your bottle of half-and-half. I want a good clear picture of one of these for our files."

"Good idea!" said Mrs. Jacobs. "Only make that *two*, would you, young man? One for me."

"How's that, ma'am?" said McGurk.

"So I can have it pinned up on the supermarket bulletin board. Asking if anyone can identify it."

McGurk brightened. "Of course, ma'am! Just what I was going to suggest myself. . . . And hold it, Officer

Bellingham! Before you go, just run your tape over this grid. I want the exact dimensions."

"What for?" asked Mrs. Jacobs.

"Because we're going to set up a replica, ma'am. And run a few tests."

It was getting late, but the following afternoon, as soon as we got back from school, we pitched right in on those tests.

And, boy, didn't it prove the value of the FTL!

For one thing, it got us thinking again about the hopping theory. Right from the start we'd had a Hopping Man on our minds. The picture of the hulking perpetrator blotted out everything else.

But when we came to try to replicate his hops in the grid drawn on the wet sand, we weren't so sure. You see, *our* prints weren't anything like so clear. The act of landing on one foot with all a person's weight behind it made a blurry print every time.

"It's more like hop*squelch* than hopscotch!" Wanda said in despair.

But McGurk's middle name isn't Perseverance for nothing. "Maybe with practice," he murmured, smoothing out the sand for the first of many repeats.

Well, after an hour or so there were fewer prints left sprawling across the lines. But even then there was still that blurriness caused by the movement of taking off and landing. And they were all much deeper at the toes than the heels.

"It's something you just can't do flat-footed, the way that guy seems to have made his," said McGurk. "Watch my left foot, men."

And, sure enough, even though he tried to *land* flat-footed, he always had to dig his toes in, ready for the spring to the next square. The result every time was a print that was heavy at the front and lighter at the heel.

"See!" he cried, just before making his turn on square number four. "It's impossible to do this flat—"

Then he came down flat-*butted* as he lost his balance.

I had to turn away to hide a grin, but some of the others couldn't keep from laughing out loud. As he began to pick himself up, crimson-faced, I thought we were in for a real bawling out.

But no. That tumble must have stirred up his brains. His face was glowing with triumph, not blazing with anger.

"Men," he declared, "we've been letting the idea of hopping run away with our imaginations! I've just tumbled—"

"You can say *that* again, McGurk!"

"Quiet, Officer Grieg! I was going to say I've just tumbled onto what really happened. Look," he said, walking back to the side of square number one. "All that guy had to do was *walk* around the edge and put his left foot, firm and flat, into each square he passed."

And he did just that. And he was right! We all took turns, and it worked every time. Six perfectly clear, flat-footed and left-footed prints per officer.

Naturally, we were pleased with the success of our experiment. Oh, yes. . . .

But when we tried to replicate the print left by that huge boot the *next* time the perpetrator struck, we came up against a much tougher problem.

It turned out to have been made already, on Tuesday night, but it wasn't until Thursday that it was discovered.

"Hey! Come and look at this!" said Wanda when she and Mari arrived at our HQ that afternoon. They were standing at the door, all excited.

"You're late!" said McGurk, frowning. "Come and look at *what*?"

"The Hopping Man—" Wanda began.

"He's done it again!" said Mari.

McGurk was out of that chair as if it were an ejector seat. "Where?"

"In the Wheelers' front yard," said Wanda. "We saw it on our way here. And talk about a *hopping* man! Wow!"

"But we've already *proved* he wasn't hopping," said McGurk. "So—"

"He was this time, Chief McGurk," said Mari.

"He just *had* to be!" said Wanda.

⑥ The Amazing Hopping Gunman?

Mr. Wheeler is definitely the kind of guy you wouldn't want to mess with.

He's short and bald and he *looks* fat—until you get near him and you can see it's mainly muscle. He hasn't been *known* to hit anyone, but if he ever does, they'll know they've *been* hit. And there's always the chance it could happen by accident, because when he sounds off he flings his arms around.

He was obviously very worked up now, at the end of his driveway. He was talking to his neighbor, Mrs. Rafferty, waving his arms and pausing every few seconds to jab a finger toward a stretch of new concrete at the side.

"He's really into small-boat sailing," Wanda had reminded us on the way.

"I know," I said. "He tows his boat around every summer, hooked onto his car. My dad hates to find himself behind him. He says he's a menace to other road users."

"Anyway, what does this have to do with the Hopping Man?" McGurk said.

"Everything," said Wanda. "Mr. Wheeler has ordered a new boat. And he wanted to have a nice new firm parking space for it."

That was when we turned the corner from Pine onto East Maple and saw Mr. Wheeler holding forth.

Mrs. Rafferty was standing at a safe distance, nodding sympathetically. There was also a crowd of kids on the sidewalk, listening.

"Gosh, look!" gasped Brains when we saw what Mr. Wheeler kept jabbing at.

It was the Hopping Man's footprint, sure enough. The size alone was enough to identify it.

But it was its position that caused some of us to gasp. I mean, there was this big oblong of fresh concrete— fifteen feet by twelve, as we soon found out. And there, without any other footprint near it, was the stamp of that huge left foot. Bang in the middle.

"Make way, please. . . ." That was McGurk, pushing his way through the crowd.

"I tell you," Mr. Wheeler was saying to Mrs. Rafferty, "we pay our taxes and what do we get when—? Uh! What do *you* want?"

He'd just missed McGurk's head by a whisker. McGurk blinked.

"We've come to investigate, sir. We're the McGurk Organization, private detectives."

"I know, I know!" growled Mr. Wheeler. "So what good do you think—"

Then he stopped. He took a deep breath and slowly nodded. "Sure," he murmured. "Why not? You can't do any worse than the police."

"Oh?" said McGurk.

"Yeah," said Mr. Wheeler. "They've *been*, all right. That dumb cop—"

"Mr. Cassidy?"

"No. Morelli. All he could say was it was probably a kid's prank. Some *kid*!"

I remembered Mrs. Jacobs had been told something similar. But I kept quiet.

"And when I told him how much it would cost," the angry taxpayer was continuing, "I mean cost in time as well as money—just to erase that—that *kid's prank* print—you know what he said?"

"No, sir," murmured McGurk. "What?"

"He said, 'Oh, I wouldn't worry about *that*, Mr. Wheeler. When you get your new boat into place there, it'll cover the print. No one will ever know it's there.'"

"Well—" McGurk began.

"As if the boat's gonna be there all the time!" howled Mr. Wheeler. "And anyway, even if it was, *I'd* know!"

McGurk nodded. "There's something else, too, sir."

"Uh—what's that, son?"

"With a person like that around," said McGurk, "—a guy who could do that to your concrete—what might he have done to your new boat if it *had* been standing there?"

Mr. Wheeler's jaw dropped. "Hey, you're right!"

"Yes, sir." Then McGurk said something he always relishes saying: "Mind if we take a look around?"

"No, go right ahead," said Mr. Wheeler. "It's set hard now. It must a been done Tuesday night when the concrete was still wet. Whoever did it put the plastic sheet back over it, real carefully. So I didn't suspect a thing until I took it off this afternoon and saw—*this*!" He gave a deep choking growl. Then he waved us on. "Go ahead," he repeated. "Take all the time you need. Though I don't think you'll find much to go on."

We went and clustered around the footprint.

There was no doubt about it. It was the same pattern and size as those on the Jacobses' patio.

Here's a close-up picture of it as it appeared on Mr. Wheeler's concrete:

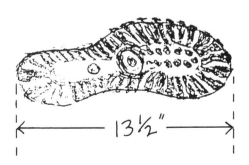

McGurk stared at it.

"But, hey . . . ," he drawled. "This time it does seem to sink deeper at the front!"

Brains was already probing the print with a blade of his Swiss Army knife, checking the depth against his tape measure. "Just over half an inch at the front," he murmured. "Uh—only three-sixteenths at the heel."

McGurk nodded. "Now, that *is* a hopping print."

"Yes, but how did it get *there*?" said Wanda. "Nobody can cover that distance in one hop, can they? And then hop the same distance clear out of it!"

I could see what she meant.

Here's the plan I made:

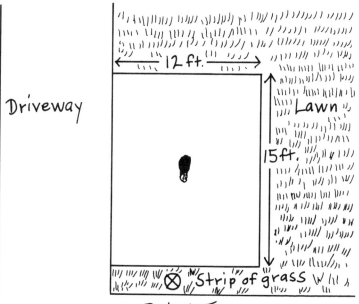

"He must have used the long route, too," said McGurk, standing on the point I've marked with an X. "From here, where he wouldn't even have room to get a good running start."

"Maybe he worked his way along the limb of a tree until he was right over the spot," said Willie. "Then he lowered his—"

"*What* limb, Willie?" said Wanda. "*What* tree?"

Willie looked around. "Uh—well—that's how he could a done it if there *was* a tree."

"How about if he used a helicopter?" said Brains, looking very sarcastic. "And got the pilot to winch him down?"

McGurk suddenly murmured, "Yeah! From above . . . maybe . . ." He started prowling across the concrete, peering down intently.

"What are you looking for, McGurk?" asked Wanda. "Splashes of aviation fuel from the helicopter?"

"No," muttered McGurk. "Holes. Probably round holes, about the size of a watch face. Like holes made by a pole digging into wet concrete."

"Are you thinking he might have *vaulted* to the center?" I said.

"Yeah," grunted McGurk. "But—uh—no sign of any holes." He sounded very disappointed.

"Maybe he could have dug the pole in at the *side* of the concrete," said Mari.

"I doubt it," said Brains, looking as if he was already figuring out directions and angles and trajectories and such.

"It's something to try out at the FTL, men," said McGurk. "But I've just had another idea. How about if he used a wide plank and laid it flat on the concrete? So it would spread his weight while he walked on it to the center. *That* wouldn't leave any footprints."

Brains frowned. "Maybe not. But the edges of the plank would leave lines as it sank in a little."

"So get down on your knees, men," said McGurk, getting down himself. "And search. Inch by inch!"

Boy, was that concrete *hard* on our knees! And all for nothing. There was no sign of any such lines anywhere.

Willie was the last to give up. He was hovering over the print itself, his nose nearly touching it.

"What is it, Officer Sandowsky?" asked McGurk. "Smell something?"

"I was hoping to, McGurk. Like maybe if he'd walked in something with a special smell. Like a bed of lavender or onions. Or—"

"But he hadn't?"

"No," said Willie. "But with getting so close I spotted this." He picked something out from one of the deeper grooves. "I thought it was a piece of grit at first. But no. It was too smooth and round and—"

"Give it to me, Officer Sandowsky!" snapped McGurk.

Then: "Well, how about *that*?" he said, as it rolled lazily on the palm of his hand. "A piece of lead shot!"

We clustered around.

"What does that tell us, Chief McGurk?" Mari asked.

"I don't know for sure. It obviously rolled there after the perp had made the print. . . ."

"It could have been dropped by anyone," I said. "Kicked there accidentally while Mr. Wheeler or Patrolman Morelli was investigating. One of *us* could have. We could have picked it up on the way here, stuck to our shoes."

"Yeah, maybe," grunted McGurk. "But suppose it had been stuck to the *perp's* boot? Or dropped from his clothes, or a pocket?"

"Well?" said Wanda.

"Well, it could mean he's used to being around shotguns," said McGurk, frowning. "Maybe even *sawed-off* shotguns!"

"Oh, boy!" I murmured.

My picture of Frankenstein's Monster was being rapidly updated. There he was—hopping around at midnight, making his massive prints, *armed with a deadly weapon*. . . .

7 Baffled

"Let's check with Mr. Wheeler," said McGurk. "Maybe *he* owns a shotgun."

But Mr. Wheeler was very positive. "My hobby's sailing. I never owned a shotgun in my life. Maybe if I did and I'd been guarding my property with it, this wouldn't have happened."

McGurk looked grave. "It's just as well you weren't, sir. You can't take the law into your—"

"Ha!" bellowed Mr. Wheeler. "Now *you're* beginning to sound like the cops! . . . Anyway, if I had been doing that, you wouldn't have found just one teeny-weeny pellet in his footprint. No, sir! There'd a been both barrels' worth in the seat of his pants!"

It was then we realized just how serious this was getting. If the perpetrator wasn't caught soon, someone might be badly hurt.

"Anyway," said Mr. Wheeler, "any clues *how* he did it?"

"We're working on it, sir," said McGurk. "We'll run some tests. Don't worry. We'll soon have it solved."

He *sounded* confident.

But whatever confidence McGurk did have soon evaporated. Hopping or vaulting (with the pole from his mother's push broom) or crawling along planks, there was no way we could plant a single clear left footprint in the sand at that distance.

"I mean, it's impossible!" McGurk kept saying. "There's no way at all!"

"Not unless he really can hop that distance," I said.

"Which would make him an Olympic record holder," said Wanda. "So all we have to do is look for someone in this town with a gold medal for the triple jump!"

I tell you, we were baffled. Absolutely baffled.

And on Friday we were *still* baffled.

By around four o'clock we were all sitting or sprawling on the grass. We'd run through all those tests again. It was a hot afternoon. We were very near exhausted.

"And just how much closer has it gotten us, McGurk?" said Wanda. "Huh?"

Even McGurk had lost his spark. "Well . . . maybe not very far."

"I mean, all we *really* know is that this time he was more careful with the plastic sheet," said Wanda.

"Oh?" muttered McGurk.

"Yeah. Like he put it back in place after he'd made his print."

Mari suddenly sat up, blinking, as if she'd just been

startled out of a deep sleep. But she didn't say anything. It was Brains who spoke next. "Maybe he wasn't in such a big hurry."

"Yeah, well," said McGurk, "it wasn't close to the house like the Jacobses' patio. Less risk of being disturbed."

And that's when Mari let out her yell. "*I have got it, Chief McGurk! I have got it!*"

It sure is funny the way the human mind works. I mean, there we'd been, exhausted. With all our ideas exhausted, too, including Mari's. Then suddenly the answer dropped into her mind, smooth and sweet and complete.

"Got *what*, Officer Yoshimura?" asked McGurk, bolt upright himself now.

"The solution!" said Mari. "I think I know how he did it!"

She got to her feet.

"Bricks, bricks!" she said. "Do you have any bricks, Chief McGurk? Loose bricks?"

"Yeah, I think so. Around by the barbecue."

"Please get them!" said Mari. "Just two will be enough!"

And you know what? She really had hit on a workable method. And you know what else? It was so *simple*.

We watched in silence as she placed one brick at one

side of the wet sand and the other opposite, at the other side.

Then she picked up one of the planks we'd spent so much time crawling along, and she lightly, *simply* placed one end of it on the first brick and the other end on the second.

"A bridge!" Willie gasped. "A footbridge!"

And so it was. Only a few inches above the surface, sure. But a few inches were all that was necessary for strolling across that plank and lowering the left foot to make your print dead center of the strip.

Which Mari did next, beaming from ear to ear.

"Well, I'll be darned!" muttered McGurk, hurrying across to try it himself.

And he was just lowering his left foot to cover Mari's print when a voice behind us said, "Practicing, McGurk?"

We all swung around.

It was Sandra Ennis. We'd been so wrapped up, we'd never even seen our old enemy come into the yard.

"Uh—what d'you *mean*, practicing?" said McGurk. "Practicing *what*?"

"Your moves," said Sandra, looking pointedly at the footprint Mari had just made. "Your steps."

"This isn't a dancing class!" said McGurk. "This is our footprint-testing laboratory!"

Sandra blinked. "Huh! That's one way of describing it, I suppose."

"What are you talking about?" said McGurk. "Describing *what*?"

"Your rehearsals for a new caper," said Sandra. "Another dumb vandal act!"

A murmur of surprise and anger arose. Wanda was already taking a step forward, fists clenched. I put a hand on her shoulder.

"Let McGurk do the talking," I said.

"Yeah!" growled McGurk, jumping off the plank. "Are you trying to say *we've* been making the footprints at the Jacobs and Wheeler houses? And are you taking this down, Officer Rockaway? Because it's one very serious accusation she's making!"

His face was crimson.

Sandra blinked again and took half a step back.

"Yes," she said. "You can't bluff your way out of *this*. I wasn't sure at first. But *now* I am. After this latest."

"What latest?"

"At the side of Mrs. Armstrong's goldfish pond. Next door to the Jacobses, on East Birch. You know very well what I'm talking about."

McGurk took a deep breath. "And what makes you think *we've* done it? Whatever it is."

"Because you had the gall to sign it, Jack McGurk, that's why. And Mrs. Armstrong has sent me to ask

you to come over. So she can confront you with your
dirty work!"

McGurk stared at his accuser, openmouthed.

Wanda took over. "*What* dirty work?"

"You know very well," Sandra said again. "Your—
uh—leader does, anyway. He's proud of it, obviously.
Ask *him*. But do it while we're on our way to Mrs. Armstrong's. Time's running out."

That sounded ominous, but McGurk was still rooted
to the spot.

"*Signed* it?" he blurted out at last. "What d'you mean,
signed it?"

"I told you—it's no use trying to bluster your way out,
McGurk. Are you coming with me or not? Mrs. Armstrong says if you don't show before four-thirty she's
going to call the police and let *them* handle it."

"Okay, okay! We're coming," said McGurk. "If only
to see what you're talking about."

"You better!" said Sandra, with a fat, smug smirk.

Even my own fingers began to curl into fists.

It was so *humiliating!* Just as if we'd *really* committed
a dreadful crime and Sandra Ennis was the arresting
officer who'd been sent to bring us in for questioning!

I *mean* . . .

Sandra Ennis! Arresting *us!*

8 McGurk Turns the Tables

For about half a block we were too stunned to speak.

Then: "What *is* this thing that we're—McGurk's—supposed to have done?" asked Wanda.

"Be quiet, Officer Grieg," said McGurk. "Wait until we see the facts for ourselves."

"Yes, be quiet, *Officer* Grieg!" said Sandra. "After all, every criminal has the right to remain silent!"

"Easy, Wanda!" I murmured. "Do as McGurk says."

So we'd all fallen silent again by the time we reached the Armstrong house.

A very tight-lipped Mrs. Armstrong was waiting in the driveway. I glanced at my watch. 4:27. We'd just made it.

"I'm sure you know where it is," she said coldly. "But I'll lead the way."

She's a thin, wiry little woman. Being a keen gardener, she's usually dressed in old jeans and heavy boots. We followed her around the back.

I'd never been there before and, I can tell you, it was something else. There were paved walkways at all levels, in and out between flower beds and low stone walls. At the end of one of these walkways was a sunken part, down five steps: a regular little oasis, surrounded by clumps of flowering bushes, with a goldfish pond in the center. The fish must have thought we'd come to feed them, because there was a seething among the lily pads as they glided to the surface. Some were more silvery than gold, plus one or two beauties with black tiger stripes.

But the stripes that very quickly grabbed our attention weren't on the fish.

The pavers around the sides were in different shapes. Some were still cracked, while others seemed to have been recently replaced. The biggest was a great rectangle of newly laid concrete, and there it was—the latest outrage. Looking like this:

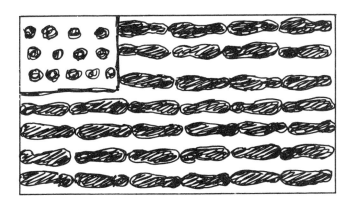

"The U.S. flag!" gasped Mari.

"Sort of," Willie murmured. "Only it doesn't have as many stars as it should."

Well, they weren't even star-*shaped.* They'd probably been made by someone dabbing and screwing the point of his or her shoe into the wet concrete. As for the stripes, they'd been formed out of footprints in continuous lines—right, left, right, and so on.

"It's a good *impression* of a U.S. flag," I said.

"A good impression of the culprit's *feet,*" said Mrs. Armstrong, staring at McGurk's. "And signed by the artist!"

She pointed to another, smaller slab a few feet to the right. It, too, had been newly laid. And there, scraped in its surface and now set hard, was this:

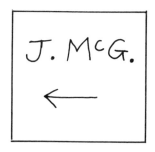

"Well, that lets *me* out anyway," said McGurk. "I mean, who'd be stupid enough to put their own initials to a criminal act?"

"*You* would!" said Sandra.

McGurk ignored her. "And if I *had* been stupid enough, it would have been J. *P.* McGurk. That's how I always sign my name, ma'am."

"Sure!" sneered Sandra. "But if he wanted people to think someone else had done it and was trying to get him blamed, this is just how a weasel-minded jerk like McGurk *would* sign it!"

"Oh, come, Sandra!" said Mrs. Armstrong, easing up a little. "Isn't that getting rather complicated?"

Sandra barreled on regardless. "Well, maybe someone *saw* him making the flag. And when he'd gone away *they* signed his name to it. So no innocent person would get blamed."

I pounced. "Why wouldn't they simply come to Mrs. Armstrong and *tell* her what they'd witnessed?"

"I—uh—don't know," said Sandra. Then: "Because they didn't want to incriminate themselves, perhaps. Yeah! Like maybe they themselves had no honest business being in here, either."

"Hey, yes!" said Willie. "Maybe someone who'd come here to steal one of these pretty fishes!"

We stared at him. He sounded just as if he were deeply impressed by Sandra's deduction!

"You're right, Willie!" she said triumphantly. "Someone like that. Someone who heard McGurk coming and hid in the bushes. Then saw him make the flag."

It was beginning to sound all too likely.

Mrs. Armstrong was looking hard at McGurk.

There was a silence, broken only by the pop-popping of the fish.

"If only they could speak!" said Mari.

But our leader hadn't been *stunned* into silence this time. He'd been busily arranging his thoughts. Not only was he having to defend himself, he was also challenged to prove who was the better detective—himself or this smirking upstart.

He turned to Mrs. Armstrong. "When did this happen, ma'am?"

"Sometime between Wednesday evening and this morning. I was visiting my sister in Queens all day yesterday. I fed the fish before going, but there was a plastic sheet over the wet concrete, so I didn't notice anything wrong. It might not have been touched yet, of course."

"So it *could* have been done in daylight?"

"Yes, well," said Mrs. Armstrong, "there's plenty of cover down here."

"Uh-huh," grunted McGurk, looking around. Then he bent to the prints. "Officer Bellingham, do you have your tape measure?"

"Sure thing, McGurk," said Brains. He ran the tape over one of the prints. "Ten inches. Exactly."

"Okay, Officer Bellingham. Now measure *mine*."

McGurk held up his foot.

"Just under nine inches," said Brains.

"Would *you* like to check that, ma'am?" McGurk asked.

Mrs. Armstrong was now looking embarrassed. "No . . . no. . . ." She faltered. "I can see. . . ."

"Those prints aren't only a different *size*," McGurk said, holding up his foot again, "but look—the pattern's totally different."

"Those down here are from Nike shoes," said Brains. "I've made a study of car tires and shoe prints."

"There you go then, ma'am!" said McGurk. "I've never owned a pair of Nikes. I'm a Reebok person myself—"

"All right, all right!" Sandra cut in. "So you could have borrowed a pair."

"A couple of sizes too big?"

"Why not?" said Sandra.

"Oh, *really*, Sandra!" Mrs. Armstrong protested.

"And what about motive, huh?" demanded McGurk. "Why would I *want* to do this?"

"To—to create a mystery!" Sandra replied. "So you could solve it and brag about it!"

"That's stupid!" I said. "How could he brag about solving it if he'd done it himself?"

"Yeah!" said Wanda. "*Some* motive!"

While this last exchange had been going on, McGurk had been stooping over the prints again. I saw him suddenly stiffen and pick up something from the "stars" corner. Something so small I couldn't see what it was.

Then he slipped it into his pocket and straightened up, just as Wanda was getting ready to let loose another volley of jeers.

"Take it easy, Officer Grieg." He turned to Mrs. Armstrong. "Ma'am, will you be having something done about this mess?"

"Of course," said Mrs. Armstrong. "I was thinking of having a thin layer of concrete put over the marks. Like the Jacobses have had done." She nodded in the direction of the house next door, hidden behind the bushes. "The young man who did Jane Ennis's driveway very kindly offered to make their pavers look like new, free of charge."

"Yes, ma'am," said McGurk. "But you won't mind if my officers take measurements and maybe take a few photos first?"

"Oh, but is there any need to go to all that trouble?"

"You bet, ma'am! Because *we're* the victims as well as you!"

"Oh?"

"Sure," said McGurk. "The motive, you see—it's obvious. To frame me—all of us—for something we didn't do!"

"Yes," said Wanda. "And I have a pretty good idea who's been doing that framing!"

"Don't look at *me*!" cried Sandra.

I must say she looked *genuinely* innocent and indignant.

But McGurk was talking to Mrs. Armstrong. "Anyway, don't worry, ma'am. The perpetrator isn't going to get away with this!"

"Well, maybe I did fly off the handle too quickly," said Mrs. Armstrong. "After all, if it *is* someone trying to get you into trouble, it's really only a childish prank. . . . A *mean* one, yes," she added, seeing the look on McGurk's face, "but basically very childish."

But McGurk hadn't been looking so stern for any selfish reason. He now threw at her what he'd thrown at Mr. Wheeler. "Childish maybe, ma'am. But a person capable of doing this has a very twisted mind. A person who might even have taken it into his head to do something bad to these goldfish!"

"Oh, my!" gasped Mrs. Armstrong. "I hadn't thought of that! Maybe I'd better call the police, after all!"

"That's your privilege, ma'am. Meanwhile, you can be assured that we'll be leaving no stone unturned in *our* investigation!"

"Neither will *I*, in *my* investigation!" blurted Sandra Ennis, flouncing off.

"That's what I call turning the tables, McGurk!" said Wanda on the way back to base.

"Huh?" he grunted. He'd been looking very thoughtful.

"Why, sure!" said Wanda. "Sandra Ennis comes hustling you in as prime suspect and ends up flouncing out with *herself* as prime suspect!"

"Right!" said Brains. "If anyone's got a motive for framing McGurk, it's *her!*"

"I'm not so sure," I said. "She looked pretty genuine when she denied it."

"Yes," said Mari. "I, too, think she was telling the truth."

Well, that was pretty conclusive to me. I mean, Mari is our voice expert. She's a first-class ventriloquist who can not only throw her own voice, but imitate other people's to a T. What's more, she can pick out every shade and tremor in someone else's voice. Our human lie detector is what McGurk often calls her.

He was nodding now. "Yes. You could be right, Officer Yoshimura."

Wanda tossed her hair. "Well *I* think Mari's wrong, for once!"

"Who *could* have done it then?" Willie asked.

"Well, it wasn't the Hopping Man this time," said Brains. "Those were ten-inch feet, not thirteen-and-a-half."

"I don't know about that, either, Officer Bellingham," McGurk said quietly.

He was fumbling with something in his shirt pocket.

I suddenly remembered. "By the way, what did you pick up off the concrete, McGurk?"

"Something very, very peculiar, Officer Rockaway. Something that tells me there's more in this concrete stomping than meets the eye!"

"What?"

He stopped and took his hand out of his pocket. "These!" he said.

And there, rolling around on the palm, were two more tiny black shotgun pellets. . . .

⑨ McGurk Gets Scared

Well, that really threw us for a loop. We'd been thinking we had two separate perpetrators to track down:

1. The massive hulk who wore 13½-inch boots.
2. A much smaller person, possibly a kid, with 10-inch feet.

But now, after McGurk's find, it was looking like there was a sinister connection.

Were they working together?

And what about the shotgun pellets?

Did they *both* go around armed?

And while this had us all perplexed, it did one thing more to McGurk. It had *him* scared; I could tell.

"Why so quiet, McGurk?" I asked the next morning in his basement. Being Saturday, we'd been planning to tour the neighborhood looking for any new strikes. But it was raining heavily, and only three of us had turned up so far.

"Huh?" he grunted. Then: "Oh—nothing. I was just thinking we'll have to wait until this rain stops."

"Come on, McGurk!" I said. "It isn't just that. You're worried, aren't you?"

He gulped. "Well, you would be, too, if you thought the Hopping Man was out to get *you*!"

Willie looked startled. "What—what d'you mean, McGurk?"

"Well, it stands to reason," he said. "I mean, the thought of another kid trying to frame me—well, that's one thing. But when I find out that some gorilla the size of the Hopping Man is in on it—some adult who's free to come and go at all hours of the night—that's different!"

I realized then that he'd probably been awake most of the night.

"Hey, yeah!" gasped Willie.

"Come on, snap out of it, fellas!" I said. "Maybe there's no connection. Maybe it was just a coincidence, finding shotgun pellets at both places."

"It doesn't *rain* shotgun pellets," said McGurk. "There *has* to be a connection."

I shrugged.

"Well, anyway, let's try a different line. Let's see if we can hit on some other possible motive. Besides framing *you*. After all, the Hopping Man himself doesn't seem to have attempted to finger you."

"No," said Willie, brightening. "*He's* just crazy, McGurk. Some kind of psycho."

That couldn't have done much for McGurk's peace of mind, but just then Brains came in. I quickly filled him in.

"Motives?" he said. "For the Hopping Man? Funnily enough, my mom and dad were talking about it last night when I got home. There've been all kinds of rumors going around about the Jacobs and Wheeler footprints. And some people are beginning to suspect the blacktop guys."

"Oh?" said McGurk.

"Yes," said Brains. "I mean, one of those guys has been going around saying that blacktop is much better at resisting pressure marks than wet concrete. And that people are dumb for not using it on their driveways."

"Go on," said McGurk. "What does this have to do with motives?"

"Well, there's nothing definite," said Brains. "But they've been saying he's really dropping hints. That for a small sum, he and his buddies might be able to let folks have bitumen left over from the road works. So they can repair their frost damage with that."

"Huh!" grunted McGurk. "That's an *old* scam!" Then he showed he still wasn't quite his usual self. "But what's that got to do with the Hopping Man prints?"

"Well," I said, "if they *are* trying to pull this scam,

that would be one way of making their point. Damaging some of the wet concrete themselves to make people switch to blacktop."

"Which they can buy from the crew cheap," said Brains.

"Yeah, well, it could figure, I guess." McGurk looked up hopefully. "Do any of those guys look like they might wear thirteen-and-a-half inch boots?"

"I don't know," I said. "I've never really taken much notice of them."

"Me either," said Willie.

"Uh-uh," said Brains.

"Are they working today?" said McGurk.

"Yes," said Brains. "And all through the weekend. It's a priority job, and—"

The door crashed open. It was Wanda and Mari, looking very wet. Wanda's hair was hanging in rattails. Usually she's fit to be tied when her hair gets like that, but today her face was glowing.

"Sorry we're late, McGurk," she said. "We've been held up again."

Mari giggled. "Yes, Chief McGurk. Held up in traffic."

"Huh? *What* traffic?"

"Well, sort of," said Wanda.

"The whole of Pine Avenue has been closed off," said Mari. "Between Maple and Birch."

"Where they've been laying blacktop," said Wanda.

"But I thought they'd finished that stretch two days ago," I said.

"They did," said Wanda. "But it isn't the road crew who've closed it off this time. It's the *police!*"

"Mr. Cassidy's car at one end," said Mari, "Patrolman Morelli's at the other."

"But *why?*" said McGurk.

"Because," said Wanda, relishing every word, "—are you ready for this?—the Hopping Man has struck again. His footprints are all over that stretch of new blacktop!"

Brains looked awestruck. "But—but he must weigh a *ton*! I mean, new blacktop, these days—it can take a *car* without showing much of a print!"

"Who said that was *how* he'd made this latest set?" Wanda replied.

"H-how then?" gasped McGurk.

"You'd better come and see for yourself, Chief McGurk," murmured Mari.

I glanced out the window. The rain was slackening off. But I don't think it would have deterred McGurk just then if it had been blowing a hurricane.

"We're on our way!" he said.

10 The Hopping Man Strikes Again

The first thing we saw was the group of men between the two patrol cars. Even though the rain had stopped, the two cops were still wearing their slickers. The other three were all members of the road crew. They'd obviously been sent for from farther along Pine Avenue. They looked all steamed up—and it wasn't because of the hot sun's action on their rain-soaked jackets.

As we drew nearer, the reason became all too plain.

For there, all over the road surface, were the unmistakable left footprints of the Hopping Man. And this time they were even more striking than those he'd made in the wet concrete.

These had all been done in white paint! Just as if he'd stepped in some huge paint can and gone crazy!

They weren't giant hops. They were more like the hops someone might make who'd just had a heavy hammer drop on his right foot and was now going around clutching that foot, staggering in agony.

Here's an impression of just a few of those prints:

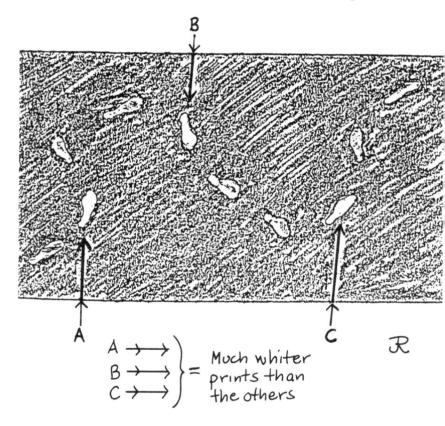

Patrolman Cassidy came over.

"It looks like a case right up your street, M'Turk," he said, getting McGurk's name wrong on purpose, as usual.

McGurk didn't bother to correct him. He was gaping at the prints.

"It's more like a case of up *everybody's* street!" growled one of the blacktop men.

"He must have used a stick for support," Wanda was saying. "Otherwise he'd have lost his balance."

"He wouldn't need a stick if he was walking normally," said Brains. "With only his left boot's sole and heel covered in paint."

"Yeah," grunted McGurk. "Good thinking, Officer Bellingham. And from the way they keep fading, it looks like he had to carry the paint can around. You know— so he could give his left boot another coat every few steps."

The men hadn't been paying much attention to us. Only when McGurk bent down and gingerly touched one of those footprints did they take any real notice.

"It's dry all right, M'Quirk," said Mr. Cassidy. "The paint is, anyway. It's only the rain that's wet."

"I'm not feeling for that," said McGurk. "You're right, Officer Bellingham. There's been no sinking in under his weight, like with the wet concrete."

"*I* could a told you that!" grumbled the road-crew boss. (McGurk took a quick look at the man's feet.) "But the prints are as bad as if they had a sunk in!" the man went on. "It looks like we're gonna have to do this whole stretch over again!"

"Yes." Mr. Cassidy looked grave. "And I suppose that's going to cost the taxpayer."

"A bundle!" growled the man. "You can bet on *that!*"

Mr. Cassidy looked at his fellow officer. "So kid's prank

or no kid's prank, Morelli, it's now gone way over the top. The lieutenant's going to want a full report."

It was nice to see Patrolman Morelli get his comeuppance.

"Don't worry, Mr. Cassidy," McGurk said. "*We're* working on it!"

"Huh!" grunted Patrolman Morelli. "I don't think Lieutenant Kaspar's gonna be thrilled to bits to hear *that*! Move out a the way and leave this to us."

McGurk didn't argue. "Sure, Mr. Morelli. . . . Come on, men."

He was looking excited. Also vastly relieved.

"What is it, McGurk?" I asked as we walked away.

"Don't you see? There might be no such person as the Hopping Man! At least, not the great hulk we've been picturing."

"Anyone who wears thirteen-and-a-half-inch boots is no midget in *my* opinion," said Brains.

"No," said McGurk. "But who says the perp *wore* them? He—or she—could have been *carrying* that left boot like you might carry a rubber date stamp."

"Hey, yes!" said Wanda.

"And he'd use the boot the same way with the wet concrete," said McGurk. "Only he didn't have to use paint for *those* prints. Just so he pressed the boot down hard enough."

"So the prints could have been made by some normal-sized person?" Wanda said eagerly. "Even a kid?"

"Sure," said McGurk—quite his usual fearless self again.

"There you go then!" said Wanda. "Sandra Ennis! She's *still* my prime suspect! I tell you, McGurk, she's been trying to frame you. Out of sheer spite."

I was beginning to think she might be right. I mean, why would the road-crew guys ruin their own blacktop? And if *that* motive didn't stand up any longer, it just had to be something like a frame-up for revenge.

"*I* think that business with the cats triggered it," said Wanda. "She was pretty riled, being shown up in front of everybody!"

And something happened within the next ten minutes that seemed to back up Wanda's theory.

We'd just reached McGurk's yard, when Mrs. McGurk emerged through the kitchen door. "I've been looking for you," she said, crossing to the garbage can and lifting its lid. "Do you know anything about these?" She pointed inside the can. "I was putting some kitchen garbage in about twenty minutes ago when I noticed them."

We stared.

Lying on top was a pair of old walking shoes, dirty and scuffed.

"Nikes!" whispered Brains.

"With dried cement on the soles!" said Wanda.

"They don't look like any of *your* shoes, Jack," said Mrs. McGurk. "Did any of you others—?"

"They *aren't* mine," said McGurk. "They're too big."

"So whose are they?" said Mrs. McGurk. "And how did they get here?"

"I don't know," said McGurk. "But I aim to find out! . . . All right, Officer Bellingham. We're taking them in for forensic examination. And be careful. There might be some shotgun pell—uh—something sticking to that cement. Embedded in it!"

11 Wanda Goes out on a Limb

Once inside the basement, McGurk placed the ratty old shoes on the table—very carefully, as though they were Cinderella's glass slippers. Then he invited Brains to sit in the rocking chair while inspecting them.

Looking very important, Brains took out his knife and began delicately prodding and scraping the cement.

The result? Negative. Just a small growing mound of powdered cement. No shotgun pellet.

"But they do measure exactly ten inches," he said at the end. "And they are Nike shoes, exactly the same pattern."

"Okay," said McGurk, looking disappointed. "You can move back to your own place now." He sat down in the vacated chair and began to rock slowly. "But one thing's definite, men. Whoever planted them in the garbage can stomped out the stars and stripes at the goldfish pond."

"Agreed," said Wanda. "And I say we go confront her

with it right now. . . . And watch her face carefully this time, Mari."

"Yes, come on, men," said McGurk. "Let's get over there now."

Sandra Ennis was walking down the front driveway when we arrived. Her hair, too, was looking wet. The gold color was darker, but the rain had made *her* hair curlier than ever.

Wanda tossed back her own damp rattails and looked at Sandra's curls with loathing. "It looks like you were out in the rain earlier," she said accusingly.

"What if I was?" said Sandra.

"You couldn't have been sneaking around outside our HQ, could you?" McGurk asked.

"Near the *garbage cans?*" Wanda added.

Sandra blinked. "I don't know what you're all gibbering about! Though as a matter of fact"—she glared at Mari—"I was just thinking of paying *you* jerks a visit."

"Oh?" said McGurk.

"Yes," sneered Sandra. "To ask a few routine questions of my own. Like where were *you*"—she glanced at Mari—"and *you*"—a glance at Wanda—"last night? Sometime after dark, it would have to be."

"What d'you mean?" said Wanda. "What are you getting at?"

"Well, I might have been getting at those paint prints

on Pine I've just heard about," said Sandra. "It seems like you *all* might have been busy last night. . . . But this is something that happened much closer. Something in *my* precinct. Three houses away. And almost opposite *your* house, Mari Yoshimura."

"What are you talking about?" said McGurk.

"Come with me and I'll *show* you," said our rival.

Well, talk about turning the tables!

It was in complete, mystified silence that we followed her to the Woodstock house and halfway up the driveway.

Despite her eagerness to find out what Sandra was talking about, I noticed that Wanda couldn't help looking up at an evergreen tree near the driveway. I'd heard her mention it before, calling it a fine specimen of a Monterey cypress.

Anyway, Sandra soon had her switching her attention to the ground.

"There!" she said. "This was patched up only yesterday. Ready for the Woodstocks' return from Florida next week. And *now* look at it!"

We stared.

A medium-sized pothole had been very neatly filled in with concrete. But it wasn't the quality of the workmanship that we were examining. It was what had been scrawled and stomped on it.

This:

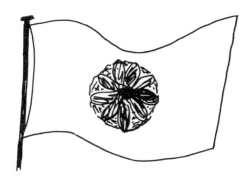

"It's a good thing Mr. and Mrs. Woodstock *are* away from home!" said Sandra.

"Who found it, then?" said McGurk.

"*I* found it," she said. "I've been asked to pick up the mail and keep an eye on their property."

"Boy!" Wanda exploded. "Talk about opportunity!"

"What's that supposed to mean?" said Sandra.

"It means, who had the perfect excuse to come in here," said Wanda. "Even in daylight!"

Sandra's eyes had a very mean gleam in them as she pointed. "Is that the Japanese flag, or is it not?"

Before anyone else could reply, Willie weighed in. "Uh—not necessarily. It could be the Bangladesh flag."

We *all* stared at him—not only Sandra.

"Are you sure, Officer Sandowsky?" asked McGurk.

"Sure," said Willie. "The Japanese and the Bangladesh flags *both* have circles in the middle. The Japanese is red on a white background. The Bangladesh is red on green."

Even Sandra was still staring.

"How d'you know all that, Willie?" asked Wanda.

Willie shook his head sadly.

"It was when I had the measles. It took away my sense of smell. I thought it had gone for good. So—so I tried to cheer myself up. By drawing all the flags of the world, then coloring them."

Wanda hurriedly brushed away a tear. "So—"

"By the time I'd gotten to Zambia my smell started to come back," said Willie. "So that was okay."

"Yes, well," said Sandra, rousing herself, "there's no doubt about *this* one. The Japanese flag. Definitely."

"What makes *you* so sure?" McGurk challenged.

Now Sandra was smirking. "Because I had a tip-off. Saying one of *you* made this."

McGurk looked startled. "What kind of tip-off? Who from?"

"It was an anonymous letter," she said. "It was in the Woodstocks' mailbox when I opened it this morning. Addressed to *me*."

"I'd like to see that letter," murmured McGurk.

"I *bet* you would!" Sandra sneered.

But then came a loud, menacing growl. Mari had been scowling down at the flag. "If you think *I* made *that*, you are very wrong!"

"Why not?" said Sandra. "*Look* at it. The outline's been drawn with a stick or something—sure. But the circle's been made by someone putting a foot there and squirming it around. You'd all have spotted that already, if you'd been *real* detectives. *I* did."

McGurk ignored the insult. "Measure it, Officer Bellingham. From the center of the circle to its outer edge."

Brains was already on it. "About four and a half inches."

"That's a pretty small shoe print, even for Mari," said McGurk.

"It could be a shoe she's grown out of," Sandra retorted.

"I did *not* do that!" Mari looked angrier and fiercer than I'd ever seen her. "I would *never* draw my country's flag on the ground for people to walk over!"

On the word "never" she stamped an admittedly small foot.

"Me either!" said McGurk, looking as if he wished he'd thought of that protest himself, back at the goldfish pond.

"Well, if it wasn't you . . ." Sandra sounded uncertain.

"*It—was—not!*" Three more stamps.

"I—I'm not saying it was," said Sandra. "It could have been a close buddy of yours. Like her. There's evidence pointing to it."

"Oh, yeah?" said Wanda.

"Yes," said Sandra, turning to the tree. "See these marks?"

She pointed to some smears of dried cement partway up a low fork. There were five of them—which I've indicated on the following diagram:

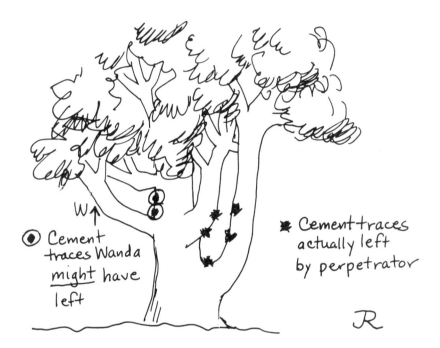

W ↑

⊙ Cement traces Wanda <u>might</u> have left

✱ Cement traces actually left by perpetrator

R

"My guess is that whoever made the flag was disturbed when a car came along the street," said Sandra. "He or *she* was afraid he or *she* would be caught in its headlights. So—being a good climber—he or *she* shinned up the tree and into the foliage."

For a few seconds, McGurk looked impressed.

But Wanda's lip was curled. "Only an *amateur* would have tried to climb by stepping onto this lower fork," she said. "It *looks* like the quickest and easiest route, sure. But it's too exposed. You'd be spotted before you'd gotten very far."

McGurk frowned. "Yes, but—"

"And these four other marks, farther up," Wanda continued, "two on each limb. Meaningless. Either he'd go up one or the other. Or flounder about hopelessly."

"What would *you* have done then?" asked Sandra.

"Easy!" jeered Wanda. "I'm taken by surprise, right? I decide to hide up in the tree, right? So the first thing I do is head for the cover of the leaves."

"So?" said Sandra.

"So I reach up to that low limb on the left, of course! And I haul myself up. And I do it fast. I don't *dangle* there. I don't hang myself out to dry for everyone to see. I swing my legs up and out of sight and plant my feet there—on the main trunk, where the branch shoots out. Which gives me the leverage to haul myself higher. Like this."

And she did exactly that. Reaching up to the limb and getting up there out of sight couldn't have taken more than ten seconds.

Sandra looked devastated. "So what are these marks all about then?" she asked.

"*I'll* tell you what they mean," said McGurk before

Wanda had time to reply. "They mean that the perp deliberately tried to frame Officer Grieg this time. *Look* at these cement marks. They're too thick. They haven't been scraped off someone's feet accidentally. The top ones are just as thick as the lower ones. Right?"

Even Sandra was having to nod her head.

"Right!" said McGurk. "*They've* been put there deliberately. Like they'd been laid on with a trowel." He started to look around. He soon pounced on a piece of broken slate. "And here's the trowel!"

Sure enough, it had been used for scraping up cement. Some was still caked on it.

"Well, don't look at *me!*" cried Sandra, completely on the defensive now. And, true to form, she went flouncing off, her cheeks burning.

But McGurk was looking at Wanda and Mari, not her.

"And now you can expect to find a pair of sneakers in *your* garbage can, Officer Yoshimura," he said gravely. "Or *yours*, Officer Grieg."

"Yeah!" said Wanda. "And that's why I'm going to keep a lookout for *her*, from now on!"

"You still think she's the perpetrator?" said McGurk.

"You're darned right I do!" said Wanda. "Like I said. She had the opportunity. And we *know* she's got the motive."

McGurk turned. "How about you, Officer Yoshimura?"

Mari was shaking her head. "I still think she was telling the truth, Chief McGurk."

"What?" yelled Wanda. "After all she's just been saying about you? Even McGurk thinks it's her now—don't you, McGurk?"

McGurk was frowning.

"Well . . . it's beginning to look that way." A few spots of rain began to rustle in the tree. "And I *am* beginning to see an overall pattern. . . . Come on. Let's go and draw up a street map showing all the hit locations. *That* should tell us something."

12 Strike Patterns and Suspects

We already had a photocopied blank of the neighborhood street plan.

"First, Officer Rockaway," said McGurk, "I want you to mark the locations of our own houses."

"Why?" asked Brains.

"Because if someone *is* trying to frame the Organization, there could be fresh strikes near *any* of our houses."

I did what he'd requested. "Now what?" I asked.

"The locations of the strikes," he said.

"Yes—but don't forget to mark Sandra Ennis's house," said Wanda.

"Good thinking, Officer Grieg," said McGurk. "Also her aunt's."

"Are we counting the cat prints as a strike?" I asked.

"No. Just the Hopping Man's and the flags."

So here is how that plan looked when I was through:

Officers' Houses
M McGurk
S Sandowsky
R Rockaway
G Grieg
Y Yoshimura
B Bellingham

Others'
SE Sandra Ennis
AJ Sandra's
Aunt Jane

Strikes
#1 (Jacobs)
#2 (Wheeler)
#3 (Armstrong)
#4 (Black top)
#5 (Woodstock)

Where I've marked the strikes with an *X*, we stuck in red thumbtacks.

"There you go then!" said Wanda. "See how they cluster around the Ennis houses!"

But McGurk was driving on. "Get out your notebook, Officer Rockaway. I want us to take a look at the probable time pattern next."

My notebook entry ended up like this:

Footprint Strikes: Probable
Time Pattern

#3 & #5 — possibly perpetrated
in daylight.

#1 — certainly after dark.

#2 —   "   "   "

(& probably in middle of night)

#4 — probably in middle of
night.

"What does *that* tell us?" asked Brains.

"It tells us that numbers one, two, and four could only have been done by adults or older kids," said McGurk. "That late at night."

"Oh, I don't know," said Wanda. "Sandra could have

snuck out while her parents were watching TV. After all, the Jacobs place is only two doors away."

"And the blacktop strike?" said McGurk. "That far from her house?"

"Sandra Ennis has gall enough for anything," said Wanda. "Especially when she's out to get someone like us."

"Well . . . maybe . . . ," McGurk murmured. Then he pointed to the Wheeler thumbtack. "But not that one. That one she could *not* do so easily—gall or no gall."

"How's that, McGurk?" asked Willie.

"Because of new information that came to light last night," said McGurk. "I didn't get around to telling you earlier, what with the blacktop business and the Japanese flag. But last night I called Mr. Wheeler to check something out."

"What was that, Chief McGurk?" asked Mari.

"About your bridge idea, Officer Yoshimura. I asked him if he'd left any loose bricks and planks lying around." He grinned.

"Well?" said Wanda.

"Well, that was one very positive guy! He said, 'I keep my yard shipshape at all times. Everything stowed away. That's why what that guy did bugged me so much!'"

"So—no planks or loose bricks?" I said.

"Loose bricks, yes. Very neatly placed at the edges of

the plastic sheet to hold it down. But definitely no planks."

"Which means—" I began.

"Which *means* that the perp must have taken along his own plank. And for that he'd need transportation. I can't see Sandra Ennis sneaking out in the dead of night and carrying a fourteen-foot plank all the way to the Wheeler driveway."

That silenced us for a while.

But Wanda never gives up, once she gets an idea in her head. "She must have done it some *other* way then!"

McGurk shrugged. "Any idea *what* other way?"

"Well . . . no . . . not at the moment."

No one else could answer that question either. After all, we'd been through it all before.

"Who else *could* it have been then?" said Wanda.

Again no answer.

"So she's the best prime suspect we've got," said Wanda. "Don't forget—it all started with the cats. Giving her the idea."

Suddenly Brains spoke up. "Hey! I've just remembered! There *was* someone else there that afternoon. An adult, too!"

McGurk shot him a keen look. "Who?"

"The guy mending Ms. Ennis's driveway. Mrs. Armstrong mentioned him fixing the damage to the Jacobses' pavers. What if *he'd* done that damage just to create a job for himself?"

Brains was obviously proud of his latest hunch. With good reason.

"Yes," I said. "And while he was doing the Jacobs repair, he'd have a great opportunity to slip into Mrs. Armstrong's garden and do some more damage."

"Exactly," said Brains. "More damage, more work. More work, more money."

"Who is he, do you know?" McGurk asked.

"Uh—no. . . ."

"Anyone?"

We all shook our heads.

"What did he *look* like then?"

No one volunteered at first. Then Brains did his best. "Uh—just a workman. Uh—baseball cap. Uh—young-ish . . ."

McGurk slapped the table. "Great! Shame on you! *What* a bunch of keen observers!"

"So what about *you*, McGurk?" said Wanda. "I suppose *you* spotted all kinds of things. Color of eyes, birthmarks, height, weight, size of *boots*. Right?"

"*I* was busy inspecting and assessing the cat's paw marks. Besides"—he suddenly brightened up—"he *might* have had a motive for stomping the Jacobses' pavers—yeah. If he'd been paid for repairing them. But the way *I* heard it, he did it as a favor. For free."

"Yes," I said. "And even if he'd accepted payment for *that*, he'd have no motive for ruining the blacktop. No one was going to offer him money for resurfacing the road."

Then it was Wanda who slapped the table. "I still think it was Sandra Ennis! I mean, what *is* this? You all seem to be dreaming up excuses and alibis for her!"

"We have to look at all possibilities, Officer Grieg," said McGurk. "But you could be on the right track. Somehow she seems to be the focus of all this. If the perp *is* someone else, he certainly seems to be using her to help pin the blame on us. Like with that anonymous tip-off."

Wanda's lip curled. "Come on, McGurk! There was no such letter. She was lying through her teeth!"

Mari looked like she was about to say something. But she sighed instead and held her peace.

"And who else hates us so much?" said Brains.

We thought of past cases and the people we'd exposed. But most of them were either in jail, or long gone from the state, or just kids who'd gotten over their gripes.

I tell you—we still seemed as far as ever from solving the mystery.

But that was before the strikes went into their final phase. The very next day . . .

13 Brains Cries "Wolf!"?

"You're late *again!*" said McGurk when Wanda and Mari arrived next morning, breathless and flushed. "This is getting to be a habit!"

"So . . . is something . . . else!" gasped Wanda.

"Not another *strike*?"

"It's . . . paint again!" said Wanda.

"On the blacktop?" said McGurk.

"No," said Wanda. "The hood of a car."

"And it is *green* paint this time, Chief McGurk," said Mari.

"*Whose* car?" said McGurk.

"The Dalys'," said Wanda. "Next door to us."

"The perpetrator walked over *that*?"

"Well, he *stood* on it, Chief McGurk," said Mari.

"Well, he or *she* stood on it," said Wanda. "So far they're all saying it was Jezebel, the golden retriever from across the road."

"Not another wrongly accused animal!" groaned Brains.

"Hold it!" said McGurk. "Are you telling me it's a *dog's* paw prints? In green *paint*?"

"Yes," said Mari. "And a *very* big dog's, Chief McGurk. I don't think it was Jezebel."

"Me either!" said Wanda. "These are *huge*!"

"As if they have been made by a monster," said Mari. "A—a *werewolf* or something!"

They both looked shaken. They most certainly *were* shaken. So shaken that Wanda hadn't even mentioned Sandra Ennis once. Or the word *cluster*.

I was reaching for the red thumbtacks, but McGurk said, "Come on, men. Let's take a look for ourselves!"

Well, those prints *were* huge.

The old brown Buick was parked on the street, and there they were, four of them—two front prints, two rear—in a standing position that straddled nearly the whole length of the hood. Here's a record of them:

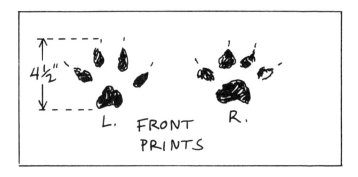

L. FRONT R.
PRINTS

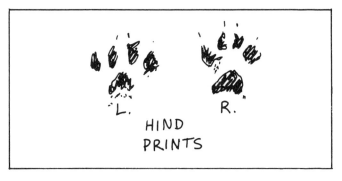

L. HIND R.
PRINTS

The hind prints were slightly smaller. The front left
came out clearest. The others were rather smudged.

As Brains was measuring the clearest and McGurk was
feeling the paint, Mrs. Daly came out.

"Someone's idea of a joke!" she said, looking mad.

"Quick-drying paint, ma'am," said McGurk. "When
was this done?"

"In the night sometime. I knew I shouldn't have left
it out here." She glanced at Wanda. "If your brother
Ed wasn't away on that survival course in Oregon, I'd
suspect *him*."

"Oh, but Ed wouldn't do anything *harmful!*" said Wanda. "I mean, the animal's *paws* would have had to be painted!"

"Obviously," said Mrs. Daly. "But the vandal would soon clean *them* up with a spot of paint remover. *This* won't come off so easily. Not without damaging the *car's* paint work. My husband's going to go bananas when he gets back from his fishing trip!"

She went back up the driveway, still shaking her head.

"Ah! Here comes the accused!" said Wanda.

It was Jezebel herself, trotting up with waving tail.

"The *wrongly* accused!" Wanda added. "Come here, honey. I bet there's not even a *speck* of paint on your paws, is there?"

"Yeah, and while we're checking for that," said McGurk, "we'll *measure* her paws, too. We'll soon clear her name."

"Excuse me, McGurk," said Brains, handing him the tape measure. "There's something I have to check on back home. I won't be long."

"Huh!" grunted McGurk. "See that you aren't, then, Officer Bellingham!"

I think McGurk suspected something that I soon began to suspect myself, after he'd passed the tape to me— that Brains had had an idea that dogs' pads could be as ticklish as folks' feet.

Because that's how it seemed. No sooner had we

started to inspect Jezebel's paws—to check for green paint, to get Willie sniffing them for evidence of paint remover, and for Guess Who to measure them—than Jezebel gave a great yelp of joy. This was followed by a whole raft of dog chuckles and giggles as she rolled over and kicked out and licked our ears.

"No trace of paint!" gasped Wanda, when she had picked herself up.

"No, Chief McGurk!" Mari confirmed, smoothing out her hair.

"No whiff of paint remover, either!" said Willie, rubbing his nose where one of Jezebel's joyously kicking back paws had grazed it.

"Well—did you get the paw measurements, Officer Rockaway?" McGurk asked.

"What *with*?" I pointed to the tape measure, which was now draped around Jezebel's neck.

She was on her feet, all braced for round two. Her tongue was lolling. She was looking at me, grinning as if to say, Come and get it, turkey! If you *can*!

"We'll never get her to calm down enough to measure her paws *now*!" I protested.

"Maybe not," said Wanda, staring down at her white shirt. "But we can measure her paw *prints*. I was just about to brush them off."

There were two of them—grimy, still slightly damp, but quite clear.

"Here, Joey!" said Mari, who'd sidled up behind Jezebel and snatched the tape free.

And that's how I got to measure Jezebel's prints.

"Just over two and one-quarter inches long," I announced.

"Well, that proves her innocence, then," said McGurk. "Good thinking, Officer Grieg."

And prove the dog's innocence that measurement certainly did!

Score: Jezebel—2¼ inches. Green Paint—4½ inches. A walkover for Green Paint in more than one way.

"C-could it be a—a German shepherd?" asked Willie.

I groaned. The idea of going through all that again was very daunting. With some strange German shepherd yet!

"No, not even that!" said a voice behind us.

It was Brains, just back, flushed and brandishing a book.

"I've been checking in this book. *One Thousand and One Animal Tracks*. And you know what?"

"What?" asked McGurk.

"I think Mari had it right the first time. Well—*nearly* right. They're *wolf* prints. The North American timber wolf. Look!"

He flipped open the book and, sure enough, under the heading, "The Crafty Gray Shadow of Our Northern Woods," there they were in black and white, matching the prints on the Buick size for size!

Our amazement lasted about five seconds. Then it turned into disbelief.

"Here? In *this* neighborhood?"

"In this *state*?"

"In this *region*, even?"

But our amazement soon crept back as we glanced from the prints on the page to those on the hood.

I mean, there was no getting away from it.

They really *did* match!

14 The Timber Wolf Strikes Again

It's a funny thing about McGurk. He loves a mystery when he's working flat out to solve it, but he hates it when everyone stands around saying how impossible it all seems.

"There's such a thing as a *tame* timber wolf!" he said. "There *are* such places as private zoos! And someone must have seen *something*. So let's get on the case, men. Door to door!"

That's why, for the rest of that Sunday morning, we went along that stretch of Oak asking if anyone had seen a person walking an extra-large dog late the previous night. (We didn't say timber wolf, of course!)

Some knew what we were getting at, having seen the car. Others looked at us as if we were crazy. The result was the same anyway. No such sighting.

But McGurk wasn't put off. Before we split up for lunch, he had us take another look at the Buick.

"Why, of *course*, men!" he yelled, almost as soon as he saw the prints again. "Forget chasing some phantom timber wolf. Just look at the prints themselves!"

They didn't look any different to me.

"Four wolf prints," said Wanda. "Yes, I see them, McGurk."

"Well that's just it, Officer Grieg! That's *all* we see. But no animal could do a vertical takeoff from the ground and land with all four feet on the hood—then take off again the same way."

"But—"

"Where are the *other* prints?" McGurk continued. "Where it scrabbled up the side and got back its balance? It's all too neat and tidy!"

"It does look pretty miraculous, now that you mention it," I murmured.

"Sure. But remember my rule, men. When something looks like a miracle, try to find out how it could have been faked!"

I didn't remember him making any such rule, but I guess he'd made it now.

"And right after lunch," he went on, "we'll run tests and see exactly how long it would take someone to *paint* those prints. By hand. As accurate and realistic as these."

We spent the whole afternoon in his basement, running those tests. We used watercolors, oil paints, finger paints, and large felt-tip pens. With Brains's book to copy from, we worked on sheets of newspaper, trying to reproduce those wolf prints accurately and swiftly. We must have used up two whole back copies of the *New York Times*'s Sunday edition.

At one point, our discarded shots littered most of the floor—and when McGurk thought he heard someone snooping around outside, he got his feet tangled up in some of those trial sheets. Anyway, there was nobody there when he opened the door, and he soon got back to work.

Well, even with uninterrupted practice, no one managed a complete set in under ten minutes. And they were all much cruder than the foursome on the Buick.

Only Willie scored any real points for accuracy. The way he applied himself to reproducing those prints in different shades of green, you'd have thought he'd gotten measles again. And when he came up with a final set, we had to step back and admire them.

"But look at the time, Officer Sandowsky!" said McGurk. "At that rate—if the perp had started in the middle of the night—it would have been dawn by the time he was through!"

"What we're looking for," said Brains, "is someone who's a very accurate, lightning-quick artist!"

"Yes," murmured McGurk. "Or someone who's clever enough to make a set of four separate rubber wolf prints. So he could daub them with paint and stamp 'em on the hood in four seconds flat—bam, bam, bam, bam!"

"It's beginning to look like an adult after all," Wanda

said reluctantly. "A fiendishly clever adult!"

"So long as it isn't a *werewolf*!" grunted Willie.

Wanda smiled sadly. "If I were you, Willie, I'd sleep with my window locked tonight. After all, it *is* a full moon."

She was joking, of course.

But she soon came to remember that many a true word is spoken in jest.

Because, that night, the timber wolf struck again!

At school the next morning, just as we were going into the classroom, Sandra Ennis dropped her bombshell.

"You've gone too far this time, McGurk!"

"Huh? What d'you—?"

"My aunt Jane's new car, too! Parked in her own driveway!"

"What about it?" said McGurk.

"You know very well! Green paw prints on the hood. Just like the Dalys' car. And I saw you all practicing making them. Yesterday afternoon when I was investigating who might have vandalized the Daly car."

That shocked us all. Not the fact that it had been Sandra who'd been snooping around, but the thought of that immaculate, beautiful white Mercedes getting the treatment!

"But I'll tell you *this*, McGurk," Sandra went on. "I know exactly *how* those prints were made."

"Huh?"

"Yes. I received another anonymous tip-off this morning. Just nine words: 'Whoever did it used a stencil on both cars.'"

We gaped at her.

"Let's see that note, then!" said Wanda.

"No way!" said Sandra. "This is *my* case now!"

McGurk seemed in a trance. "A—a *stencil*?"

"Yes, and it checks out!" said Sandra. "I went out and measured the prints on Aunt Jane's car and then ran over to the Dalys. And they fit. Look!"

She thrust out a notebook.

Well, here's a photocopy of *her* notes, which we obtained later. That copycat creep had even used the same kind of notebook as *mine*!

Aunt Jane's Car

Distance between 2 front paws = 7⅛"

Distance between 2 back paws = 5¼"

Distance between front + back
paws = 30"

Mr. & Mrs. Daly's Car

All three measurements
exactly same!!!

I don't know how McGurk managed to get through the rest of that day in school. He went around like he'd been poleaxed.

But I knew why.

It wasn't so much Sandra Ennis's sly semiaccusation that *he'd* masterminded those stencil prints. It was the fact that she'd come up with the most likely explanation when *he* hadn't. She'd beaten him at his own game!

I tried to console him. "Don't take it so *hard*, McGurk. After all, *she'd* been tipped off."

"I don't care," he said. "I should a thought of it myself!"

As soon as we got out of school, we made a beeline for Ms. Ennis's driveway. But the Mercedes wasn't there, so we went straight to the Daly house instead. Fortunately, the Buick was still out on the street.

"Yeah," McGurk murmured, looking at the prints. "It could have been a stencil. Four cutout prints on a roll of tough paper or plastic. Spread the roll out"—he went through the motions with an invisible roll—"then brush on the paint. All done in about three seconds."

"It certainly beats having to make a set of rubber stamps, McGurk," said Brains.

"Yeah, well—you win a few and you lose a few, Officer Bellingham. And don't just stand there. Check her measurements!"

As Brains got busy and started murmuring, "Yeah,

that's correct," and "Yeah, she got that one right," McGurk winced and turned his head away. I guessed he just couldn't bear the sight and sound of Sandra's being proved so right by one of his own officers.

Then he stiffened. Something on the windshield had caught his eye. He reached out and carefully plucked at a hair that had been snagged in one of the wipers. It was a long, coarse, silvery gray hair, black at one end.

And now his green eyes went into a glittery dance routine, darting between the wiper and the nearest paw prints—the hind ones. Then: "Hey!" he roared. "Look at *this*! I'm no expert, but if this hair doesn't come from a timber wolf's tail, I'll eat my magnifying glass!"

I stared at the hood. I tried to picture one of those Crafty Gray Shadows of Our Northern Woods standing there in the moonlight, green-footed, with its tail brushing the windshield. It wasn't all that difficult.

"But, McGurk," I said, "we've already ruled out a live animal and—"

"Live animal, my foot! How about a *stuffed* animal? A stuffed wolf with green paint daubed on its feet? It not only beats a set of rubber stamps, Officer Bellingham. It beats a set of crummy stencil prints, too!"

"But a stuffed *wolf*, McGurk!" Wanda began. "Where—?"

"The town museum, that's where!" he said. "Let's

check it out, men. Let's see if they've had one missing recently."

Well, I must say we'd never known a case like this, with the strikes getting weirder and weirder and finally coming so thick and fast. We hadn't even begun to investigate this latest hunch of McGurk's before we were confronted with yet another outrage.

I mean, there we were, hurrying along Pine near the corner of Maple, when we were arrested by a roar of, "Hey! Come here! Quick!"

It was Mr. Wheeler, waving his arms at the end of his driveway.

"We're busy right now, sir," McGurk called back. "And—"

"Not too busy to see *this*, I hope! My concrete strip's been hit again!"

That got to McGurk. "Don't tell me, sir," he said, as we went hurrying toward the Wheeler driveway. "A wolf with green paint on its paws!"

"A w—?" Mr. Wheeler broke off. "You gone nuts or something? I'm talking about *this*! *This!*"

We looked down to where he was pointing. And as we gaped, we gasped.

All thoughts of timber wolves flew right out of my head.

Because—well, look. Here's the drawing I made for our records, complete with Brains's measurements:

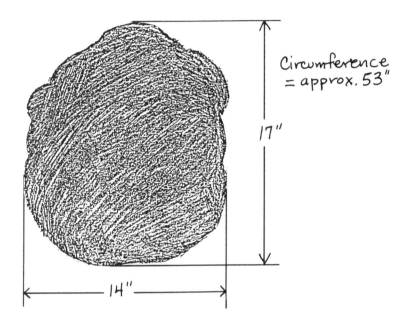

Circumference = approx. 53"

17"

14"

This one had been deeply impressed in a patch of newly laid concrete where the Hopping Man's print had been.

Already Brains was on his knees taking measurements.

Mr. Wheeler was clutching a plastic sheet.

"I'd only just taken this off to see if it was setting all right. I had a guy chisel out that footprint and fill it with new concrete. And now this! It—it looks like he stood a *barrel* on it or something!"

Brains looked up. His face was a picture of awe.

"This was no barrel, sir. This—I've been studying animal tracks—uh—right, McGurk?"

"Right, right, Officer Bellingham! So what does this one—?"

"A—an *elephant's* print!" said Brains. "The front foot of a full-size African elephant, I swear it!"

"Officer Bellingham, if this is your idea of a joke—"

"Yeah!" growled Mr. Wheeler.

"No!" gasped Brains. "Honestly! I—" His eyes had strayed to something a few feet away. He pounced on it. I thought it was a piece of charred brown paper at first, but it was much more substantial, as I soon saw.

Brains looked very excited now. "There! Just take a look at this! Animal hide. *Elephant* hide! Come from between two of its toenails by the looks of it!"

And sure enough, that's just what it seemed to be. Triangular, scuffed, and raggedy toward the point, but torn off more neatly across the top. Like this:

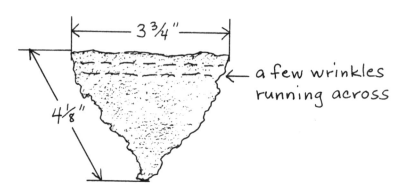

Wanda spoke first. While everyone else was looking dumbfounded, she groaned and said, "Great! So all we're looking for now is a one-legged, full-grown African elephant with a *hangnail* problem!"

15 McGurk Puts His Foot Down

That elephant's footprint was the last straw for McGurk. In fact, it nearly caused the breakup of the Organization.

"Be quiet, Officer Grieg!" he said, red-faced. "You're probably right, Mr. Wheeler. It does look like it was made with a barrel or tub or something. This bit of leather may have nothing to do with it—but we'll take it just in case. . . . And *you* be quiet, Officer Bellingham! You're letting your imagination run haywire!"

"But I tell you—"

"Not now!" snapped McGurk. "We've got to run before the museum closes. We'll get back to you, Mr. Wheeler. Don't worry."

As we hurried away, I thought I could see the reason for McGurk's annoyance. He'd had his heart set on following up the stuffed-wolf clue, and this elephant print had suddenly gotten in his way. He probably suspected our science expert of deliberately hyping up the new strike.

And it did seem to look like that.

Nearly all the way to the museum, Brains went on and on and *on* about that print. He even whipped out his calculator and started making calculations about the elephant's overall size.

"I was reading about it only last night," he said, stabbing away at the numbers as he trotted along. "Twice the circumference of its foot . . . that's two times fifty-three . . . that's one hundred six . . . plus ten percent . . . that's one hundred six plus ten point six . . . that's one hundred sixteen point six inches. And *that* is—hey!"

He stopped. "That's over nine feet eight inches!"

"What is?" I asked.

"The height of the elephant's shoulder from the ground. That's *huge!*"

"Officer Bellingham!" said McGurk, looking furious. "One more word about that elephant—that alleged elephant—that *phantom* elephant—and I'll bust you! . . . Now, come on."

So Brains kept quiet after that—or at least made sure McGurk didn't hear him.

Because his elephant really had grabbed our imaginations.

Willie kept asking if it was really that big.

"Well, you saw its footprint," Brains muttered.

"Yeah, I know," said Willie. "But wow! Nine feet eight inches!"

"Sure," muttered Brains. "And some—uh—you-know-whats are even bigger."

Even Wanda looked impressed.

"Hey, Brains!" said Willie, when we'd nearly reached the museum. "Do they ever have stuffed *elephants*?"

"In some of the larger museums, yes. Like in . . ." Brains faltered. McGurk had turned and was glaring at Willie.

"I *heard* that, Officer Sandowsky! . . . And I'll let it pass this once. But if you or anyone else dares to mention stuffed elephants or elephant footprints in *there* . . . well, you know what to expect. *First*, they'll laugh us out of the building. And *second*, I'll pull your Organization ID cards!"

Inside, we left most of the talking to him.

"Stuffed timber wolf?" asked Joanne Cooper, the assistant curator and an old friend of ours. "Well, no. Why do you ask? A school project?"

"No," said McGurk. "Someone's been fooling around, leaving timber-wolf prints. Some kind of hoax. *I* think it's probably a stuffed one."

Joanne laughed. "It better not be a *live* one!" Then she became serious. "We did have a stuffed *red* wolf once. But we got rid of it years ago. Its fur started dropping out."

"Got rid of it?" said McGurk. "Where?"

Joanne shook her head. "I don't remember. Dump, I suppose. Anyway, the red wolf is smaller. You sure these were timber-wolf prints?"

"Positive!" said Brains.

McGurk gave him a warning frown. "Have you any idea where they *might* have stuffed timber wolves, Joanne?"

"Well, in some of the larger museums, probably—"

Joanne didn't get to finish.

Her last words so closely echoed what Brains had been saying to Willie a few minutes earlier that it must have released a trigger in Willie's mind. Before he could stop himself, he blurted out, "Do they have stuffed *elephants*, Joanne? I mean in—"

"*Officer Sandowsky!*" McGurk was glaring at him.

Joanne laughed. "Don't tell me someone's been leaving elephant footprints for a hoax!"

Then *Brains* blurted out, "Well, yes. Just one. A single elephant footprint!"

McGurk's face was scarlet.

But then Joanne said something that riveted him. "Oh, well—they wouldn't need a whole stuffed elephant for *that*!"

"Oh?"

"Why, no," said Joanne. "All they'd need was an elephant's-foot umbrella stand." She made a face. "Yes, it's true! They used to make them out of elephants' feet. Just for dumping umbrellas in! We had one of *them* once, too. But you won't find them in any self-respecting town museum today!"

"Where then?" asked McGurk, fingers crossed.

"Oh . . . in the attics of some older homes, maybe. And in so-called antiques shops. There are probably one or two right here in town. And of course, an antiques shop is just the place to look for the odd stuffed animal, too."

We were out of there in two minutes flat.

"It's too late now, men," said McGurk, as the library clock struck five-thirty. "But tomorrow, after school, we start checking with every antiques dealer in town. Meanwhile, Officer Rockaway will be drawing up a list from the yellow pages."

He put a hand on Brains's shoulder. We were standing close to the War Memorial by then. His expression was grave but kindly. He looked just like he was going to pin a medal on our science expert.

"You think that really *was* a genuine elephant's footprint then, Officer Bellingham?"

"Yes . . . uh . . . sure. . . ." Brains muttered warily.

McGurk's hand rose and fell in an unmistakable pat.

"Nice work, Officer Bellingham! . . . And Officer San-dowsky—" Willie flinched as McGurk swung to face him. "You, too! That was one very good question! It might just have helped to sew up the whole case!"

I tell you—once McGurk gets a lead like that, he's all heart. For helping to put him onto it, he'll forgive anyone almost anything!

16 McGurk Gets the Boot

When we met up in the school yard the next morning, I had my list ready.

"It's rather a long one, McGurk," I said. "It could take us weeks—"

"Never mind that, Officer Rockaway," he said. "Look what I got in the mail!" He pulled out an envelope. "Addressed to *Master* J. McGurk," he said. "I *hate* being addressed as that. But that isn't the point. This *is*." He slipped the piece of paper out of the envelope. "Gather around, all of you. And don't let anyone else see it."

"It's an anonymous note!" said Wanda, staring at the message on the cheap blue paper.

And it sure was! A few lines in what looked like heavily disguised printing. Here's a photocopy:

SANDRA ENNIS HAS HIDDEN INCRIMINATING
EVIDENCE IN HER FRONT YARD. SMALL
BLACK PLASTIC BUNDLE UNDER SECOND
BUSH FROM LEFT CLOSE TO FENCE,
ONLY TEMPORARY — SO HURRY BEFORE
SHE DESTROYS IT.

"As soon as we're free, men, that's where we're heading!" he said.

Well, this turned out to be another day when the education department's money and energies were wasted on McGurk. And on most of the rest of us, too. We could hardly wait to get our hands on that "incriminating evidence."

Wanda especially. "Looks like I was right all along, McGurk," she said when, shortly after two-thirty, we crossed Oak Avenue to Sandra's house.

And it did begin to look that way. Because there, just over the picket fence, under the second laurel bush, we saw it. A small black plastic bundle, half hidden under some dead leaves.

McGurk hesitated. It was just too far to reach from the sidewalk.

"We really ought to have some kind of search warrant before—"

"Oh, get out of the way!" said Wanda. "Pussyfooting! If it was a ball we'd thrown there accidentally, we'd have gone in and got it by now."

And in another second she was crouched under the bush, brushing the leaves off the parcel. "I don't know what's inside, but it feels like—*oh!*"

We'd forgotten about the Silent Sentinel.

But all of a sudden, there Tweelak *was*, sitting on

Wanda's back, squeezing her eyes and digging her claws in whenever Wanda made the slightest move.

"Well, don't just stand there!" Wanda pleaded. "Come and get it off me!"

And even as Mari was getting ready to go to the rescue, a voice behind us said, "Hey! What are you doing in my yard?"

"Being assaulted by your cat!" said Wanda. "Here! Catch, McGurk!"

Sandra was already over the fence, reaching down to the cat. She seemed more concerned about that than about intercepting the parcel as it flew past her.

But she quickly got interested.

"What's that?" she said, nursing the cat and allowing Wanda to stand up.

"We'll soon see," muttered McGurk, unraveling the bag. "It feels like—it *is*! It's a *boot*! *The* boot! It has to be—look at this!"

Well, a boot it most certainly was. A very large, brown, dirty work boot, laced up. And as McGurk turned it over, pointing to the white paint on the sole and heel and to the very familiar pattern already pictured in our records and on the supermarket bulletin board—not to mention imprinted on six pavers, a large concrete strip, and a stretch of blacktop—even Sandra knew what it was.

"What's it doing *here*?" she gasped.

"That's what we're expecting *you* to tell *us*!" said Wanda.

McGurk was studying two crude holes in the sides of the boot. Here's a rough sketch, showing them:

Hole #1
(#2 on other side)

"But—but I've never *seen* it before!"

"That's what they all say," said Wanda.

"Check the measurement, Officer Bellingham," said McGurk.

Sandra made a grab for it. "It was in *my* yard and—"

"Sure," said Wanda. "In *your* yard!"

Sandra quickly drew back her hand.

"Thirteen and one-half inches, McGurk," said Brains. "It's the Hopping Man's right enough!"

Sandra's face twisted up. "You—you planted it there! You're trying to get me blamed for it! You—I'm going to fetch my mother!"

"Hold it!" said McGurk. "*We* didn't plant it there. Whoever did is the one who wrote this."

Sandra blinked at the envelope. "What is it?"

"An anonymous note," said McGurk. "Like the ones you've been getting, I bet." He read it out loud.

"Let *me* see that!" said Sandra.

"Uh-uh!" grunted McGurk. "Let *us* see *yours*. Then we'll share them."

Sandra's blue eyes smoldered angrily. She tossed her golden curls, said, "Oh, all right!"—and flounced off.

"Come on, McGurk!" said Wanda. "Let's take the boot straight to the police. She's only stalling for time."

McGurk shook his head. "I don't think so. I think she was genuinely surprised."

"I, too, Chief McGurk," said Mari.

"Oh, well!" Wanda tossed *her* hair. "If you want to let her off the hook—"

But by then Sandra was back, with two pieces of paper, both blue. She exchanged them with McGurk's.

"Same kind of printing," she said.

"Yeah!" grunted McGurk. "Exactly."

We bent our heads to the notes that Sandra had received. Here are photocopies of *them*:

#1) SOMEONE HAS PLANTED JAPANESE
FLAG IN WOODSTOCK DRIVEWAY,
ASK McGURK & CO. WHAT THEY
KNOW ABOUT IT!

#2) WHOEVER DID IT USED A STENCIL
ON BOTH CARS.

"Hm!" murmured McGurk. "Looks like someone's been playing both ends against the middle."

Sandra seemed to be just about to agree when her mother's voice broke in. "Sandra! You'll be late for your dancing class!"

"Coming, Mom!" she called back. "What are you going to do with the boot?" she asked McGurk.

"Keep it for further examination."

"You—you won't be running to the police with it?"

"Unfortunately, it seems *not!*" said Wanda.

"Not yet, anyway," said McGurk. "We have one or two points to check up on. But don't worry. You're no longer a prime suspect. Uh—we'll hold onto your notes, too—okay?"

Sandra frowned. "But they were addressed to *me!* And—"

"Sandra!" her mother's voice rang out.

"Oh, all right then!" she said to McGurk, hurrying off.

"So what about those holes, McGurk?" said Brains. "Looks like they've been made by someone hacking with a knife."

"Yeah!" said Willie. "Like my granddad's shoes. Only he made his extra holes at the toe end. He has bunions."

"Yes, Officer Sandowsky." McGurk was groping inside the boot. "But—"

"I mean the guy who made these," Willie went on, "maybe he has oversize anklebones. Or—hey!—maybe he has bunions on his *ankles*!"

"Oh, boy!" groaned Wanda. "First an elephant with a hangnail, now a giant with bunions on his ankles! This is getting—" She broke off. "What's up *now*, McGurk?"

"It's what's *down*, Officer Grieg," he said, his eyes gleaming. "Deep down. In here. Wedged between the upper and the sole."

Then he drew out his hand, and there, pinched between finger and thumb, was another shotgun pellet!

"Anyway," he said, "we'll puzzle over this later. Let's get on with our tour of the antiques shops."

17 Bob's Bric-a-Brac

We got lucky that day. Bob's Bric-a-Brac was only the second on that long list. We found it at the end of a dingy side street.

"Well, let's go in then, if we're going!" said Wanda.

McGurk grunted. He was peering at the OPEN sign on the door.

I guessed he was still smarting after our brush with the owner of Acme Antiques. She'd looked at us as if we'd crept out of the wormholes in the ancient three-thousand-dollar writing desk in her window. "Stuffed *wolves*? Elephant-foot *umbrella stands*? You've come to the wrong place, sonny. Try the dump."

Well, *Bob's* didn't look like the wrong place. *His* window looked like it might *be* the dump. Old clothes, tarnished spoons, broken dolls, a 1930s radio, a deep-sea diver's helmet of the earliest design, with no glass in its visor. . . . The only thing that didn't look old was the U.S. flag draped behind them, screening the window from the rest of the store. A card said in tiny printing that it was a *replica* of the Union's first flag.

"Interesting!" murmured McGurk, glancing at this. Then he opened the door.

It was dark in there and crowded with more junk: heavy pieces of furniture; bundles of rusty farming tools—pitchforks, manure hooks, hoes—and what looked like bamboo curtain poles, leaning against the walls; a faceless grandfather clock; some bookcases, their shelves loaded with old candlesticks and chipped plates and cups instead of books. One big, murky, muddled mess.

Then out of the murk stepped this tall, thin guy. He was going bald but didn't look very old. What he *did* look was uneasy. Very uneasy.

"Can I help you?" he said, smiling nervously.

"Yes, sir," said our leader. "We're the McGurk Organization, private detectives—"

"Oh!" The man's smile vanished. "If it's about the newspaper articles telling people to beware of fake antiques, you're wasting your time."

"Well, as a matter of fact, sir—"

"Everything on sale here is honestly labeled. As you can see."

Well, there were certainly plenty of hand-printed labels. I peered closer at some of the nearest. Words like *genuine, replica, solid teak, rosewood veneer* . . .

Even McGurk seemed interested in checking them out.

The man rattled on, "I might tell you that *some* dealers would try to pass off that flag as an original seventeen seventy-seven Union fl—"

"Yes, sir," McGurk cut in. "But we're more interested in something else."

"Uh—like what?" said the man, uneasy again.

"Stuffed wolves," said McGurk. "Elephant-foot umbrella stands—"

"There's one here!" said Willie, who'd been snooping around, sniffing.

Well, it *was* dark in there, but our eyes were getting used to it. And what we saw, behind a pile of old oak sap buckets, made some of us catch our breaths.

Yes. Tublike, sure. Almost like a big sap bucket itself. But there was no mistaking that grayish brown skin and the large, curved, amber toenails. McGurk pulled it away from the corner as if to admire the surprisingly delicate wrinkles in a better light. But, as he told us later, he was really taking a closer look at the skin between those nails. And, sure enough, there was a missing patch, triangular, about four inches long.

"I'm afraid it isn't for sale," said the man.

McGurk was now fumbling under the bottom of the

foot. "Hm!" he murmured, removing his hand and looking at something gray and crumbly, which could only have been dried cement.

"Yes, yes," said the dealer. "It's in very bad condition, dropping to pieces. That's why—"

"*Hey! And here's a wolf!*" said Willie.

He was now bending down behind an old butter churn, sniffing like mad.

The man spun around, but we were already surging past him.

And there was no mistaking what *that* was. In the dim light it looked even longer and bulkier than I'd expected. It had certainly been a timber wolf at one time.

"It is very big!" whispered Mari, sounding awed.

"And in pretty bad shape!" said Brains.

One of its glass eyes was missing. The left ear was collapsed, crumpled. The wire that had once helped the ear to be pricked up was now sticking out, bare. The lower jaw had collapsed, too, and was hanging down loose, supported only by *its* wire.

There was something very similar happening to the man just then. That guy's jaw really had dropped.

But he quickly recovered. "Why, yes," he babbled, "the gray wolf, also known as the timber wolf, yes, *Canis lupus*, that's its Latin name. Yes. I picked it up in Massachusetts. It had been in a museum diorama, but—" He broke off. "What's *he* doing?" he croaked.

Willie had turned the beast upside down and was sniffing its paws. There was no green paint on them that *I* could see. But Willie had no doubts about what he could smell.

"Oil of turpentine! These have been wiped with turps! Recently, too!"

McGurk looked up. "Mr.—uh—Bob—could it have been because there was green paint on them?"

"Well—uh—green paint? Uh—*green*—uh?" The dealer had been pressing his hands together and twisting his fingers around. Then his shoulders sagged and he sat down heavily on an old sea chest.

"Oh, all right!" he said. "I guess you're inquiring about the paw marks on those cars, huh?"

We looked at one another, hardly able to believe our luck.

"Yes, sir," said McGurk.

"Well, I might as well come clean," said the man. "I didn't want to get her into trouble. But she did borrow the wolf, yes. And the umbrella stand. She told me she wanted to show her teacher. Something about a project on endangered species."

"Who, sir?" murmured McGurk.

The man sighed. "My cousin. Kid your age. A cute little girl, but kind of pushy—"

"Sandra Ennis!" Wanda blurted out.

The man nodded miserably. "I never dreamed she

wanted to use them to do so much damage!"

Wanda drew in a quick breath. Then she shut her mouth and kept it shut.

"Uh—what are you going to do now?" Cousin Bob asked anxiously.

"Confront her with it!" our leader said sternly. "Interrogate her. See if she can wriggle her way out of *this*!"

As we turned to go, Bob stood up. "You—you won't tell her I told you all this, will you? I mean she *is* family and—"

"Don't worry, sir," said McGurk. "We always try to keep the identity of our informants confidential."

Outside in the street, McGurk stopped. He was fumbling in his pockets.

I couldn't help it—I just had to ask him straight out: "You didn't buy that about Sandra, did you? I mean, you saw the *size* of that wolf—"

"Of *course* I didn't buy it, Officer Rockaway!"

"I could *tell* he wasn't speaking the truth, Chief McGurk!" said Mari.

"So could I," grunted Wanda. "Much as I hate to admit it. He'd been taken completely by surprise and he was making things up as he went along."

"Yes," said McGurk. "But there was something else, besides his manner. Two things, in fact. One: The way he pretended not to know who we were when we first went in."

"Well, maybe he didn't," said Brains.

"But he *did*, Officer Bellingham! Because *he* was the guy who was repairing Ms. Ennis's driveway the day we cleared Whiskers's name. He'd actually seen us in action then. Heard our names. Must have."

"Are you sure, McGurk?" I asked.

I was trying to visualize the man in the baseball cap, but it was still too vague. The others seemed just as doubtful.

"Yes. Positive," he said. "Which brings me to the second thing. Remember that notice in Ms. Ennis's driveway? Warning people to keep off the wet concrete?"

Well, now he was talking words. And words I do observe. Especially when there's something unusual about them.

"Yes. 'Wet Concrete. Please Keep Off.' . . . With Greek *E*s."

"What are Greek *E*s?" said Willie.

"Like all the *E*s on the labels in *there*!" said McGurk. "*Replica. Genuine.* All those."

"Gosh, yes!" I gasped.

"And like all the *E*s that he nearly forgot to disguise in these notes," said McGurk, pulling them out.

He pointed to where the letter *E* had been changed.

I made a note of this later. Here it is:

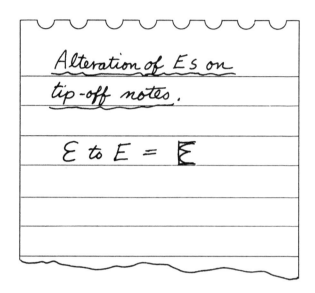

"So *he* sent those notes!" said Brains. "But why?"

Before McGurk could reply, Mari plucked his sleeve. "Be careful, Chief McGurk! He may be watching—"

"That's just what I hope he's doing," said McGurk grimly. "Maybe he'll panic and make a *really* big mistake!"

Well, I for one am *sure* that guy must have been watching. And I'm also pretty sure he *was* beginning to panic.

Because when Willie, having seen only the altered *E*s in the notes, said, "I *still* don't know what a Greek *E* is!" McGurk said, "Come over here and I'll show you the one that alerted me before we went in. On this OPEN notice." But when we went up to look at it, that notice had been sneakily turned around and now read:

"So what do we do now, McGurk?" Wanda asked.

"What we said we'd do," said McGurk. "We go and interrogate Sandra. But about *him*, not her."

18 Cousin Bob

Sandra had returned from her dancing class. She was peering under the bushes.

"Oh, hi!" she said. "I was just looking to see if anything else had been stashed here."

"*Have* you found anything?" McGurk asked.

"No. . . . Have *you* discovered anything else?"

"Maybe," said McGurk. "But we need to ask you a few questions first."

"Well, keep your voices down." Sandra glanced across to Ms. Ennis's driveway, where her aunt was deep in conversation with Mrs. Jacobs. I caught a snatch of what Ms. Ennis was saying: ". . . concrete bad enough, but *paint!*"

"My aunt's terribly upset," murmured Sandra. "She's been going on and on about vandals. If she thought I was even *suspected*"—Sandra shuddered—"I'd be in deep, deep trouble!"

"Even for the less serious strikes?" said McGurk. "Like the flags?"

"Yeah!" growled Wanda, giving her former prime suspect a hard look.

"Even for them!" said Sandra. "And *please* keep your voices down. She'd never speak to me again. She'd disown me like she . . ."

"Go on," said McGurk. "Like she *what*?"

"Oh, nothing. An old family matter."

"Talking of family," said McGurk, "who was that guy who was repairing her driveway? When the cats—"

"Oh, *him*!" said Sandra. "Yes. That was my cousin."

"The guy who owns an antiques store downtown?"

Sandra sniffed. "If you can call it that. My mother says it's nothing more than a glorified garage sale."

"You've never been there yourself?" asked McGurk.

"Me? Why would I? I like *nice* old things; pretty things."

"But he seemed like a nice kind of guy. Helping your aunt with her driveway."

"Oh, sure!" said Sandra. "Your friendly neighborhood Good Samaritan! Ever since he turned up again, a year ago, he's been doing his best to crawl his way back into her good graces."

"What d'you mean, 'crawl his way back'?"

"Well, he was her fair-haired boy at one time," said Sandra. "She brought him up after his parents were killed in a fire. From the age of ten to eighteen she treated him like her own son. Her *only* son. And heir."

"What happened when he was eighteen?" McGurk asked.

"She found him out. He'd been robbing her blind for years. Housekeeping money at first. A few dollars here, a few dollars there. But then he got greedy and her jewelry started to melt away."

"So what happened?"

"She threw him out. She threw him out of her house and cut him out of her will. I was only a baby, but my mom's told me all about it."

McGurk was looking *very* interested now. "When did he turn up again?"

"I *told* you. About a year ago. Nothing had been heard of him for all those years, and then he showed up. Opened up that stupid store and told her how he'd re-formed and was now making a good honest living. Also how he was oh-so-sorry for what he'd done."

"And she forgave him, huh?" said Wanda.

Sandra gave a thin smile. "Well—my aunt Jane isn't the forgiving kind. But the way he's kept coming on, doing odd jobs for her and bringing her flowers on Mother's Day"—Sandra's smile had faded—"I guess she's started softening up some."

"And put him back in her will?" said McGurk.

"Oh, no! Not that!" Sandra said quickly. "*I'm* her favorite young relative now. My mother knows for a fact that Aunt Jane's leaving all her money to *me*—which is why—"

"Sure, sure," said McGurk, looking *extremely* thoughtful.

Sandra checked herself. "Anyway, what else have you found out about these"—she glanced across and lowered her voice—"these vandal acts? Because the sooner we uncover the real culprit or culprits, the better."

"We're getting there," said McGurk. His eyes were gleaming. "In fact, I think I can now guarantee to have put the whole picture together by tomorrow afternoon."

I looked at him sharply, wondering why he sounded so sure.

"Tomorrow afternoon?" said Sandra.

"Yes," he said. "At three o'clock in the McGurk Organization HQ. Can you be there?"

"I—well—" Sandra looked uncertain. Then her aunt's angry voice drifted across: ". . . far too *lenient* with them nowadays! If I had *my* way . . ."

"You bet I can!" Sandra said. "Three o'clock. And it better be good!"

After that, McGurk remained absolutely stubborn about the details.

"Have you *really* solved it, McGurk?" I asked.

"You'll find out, Officer Rockaway."

"Was it Bob?"

"You'll find out, Officer Sandowsky."

"Did Sandra Ennis do *any* of it? Like the Japa-nese fl—"

"You'll find out, Officer Grieg."

"What are you going to do next, Chief McGurk?"

"Go home," he said. "Have my supper, do some think-ing, and get a good night's sleep. I still have one or two final points to clear up."

Well, I hoped he knew what he was doing. The way he was acting (in his favorite role: The Big Detective Gets Ready to Reveal Everything) he was going to look pretty foolish if he didn't deliver on time at that very special meeting!

19 McGurk Reveals All—Almost

We were all on time the next day, but McGurk made us wait outside a few minutes.

"Until I've finished getting the place ready," he explained.

As far as I could see, when we went in, this meant: (1) putting the cardboard box labeled EVIDENCE on the table and (2) adding a kitchen stool to the chairs.

"You take the stool, Officer Bellingham," he said, "and let our client have your chair."

"*Client?*" said Wanda and Sandra simultaneously.

Well, we were *all* taken aback. The idea of Sandra Ennis being a client of the McGurk Organization seemed as big a flip-flop as if Batman had gone to the aid of the Penguin!

"Yes," said McGurk. "And by the time I'm through, she'll be our *grateful* client."

"Sandra Ennis? Grateful?" said Wanda. "Give me a break!"

"I didn't come here to be insulted!" said Sandra.

"Sit down, miss!" growled McGurk. "If you want to find out just how close you are to being the victim of a fiendishly cunning scheme! A scheme that might easily have ended in murder!"

The word *murder* and the horribly squinty way he said it had both Sandra and Wanda quickly settling into their seats.

Then, gazing dreamily over our heads, he began. "What we have here, men—and client—is a brand-new type of crime. Frame-ups of people for things they haven't done are a dime a dozen. But this has been a *double* frame-up. A fake frame-up leading to the real frame-up. Leaving the true perpetrator right outside the picture—looking totally innocent and unsuspected."

"You mean—?" Sandra began.

"Your cousin Bob, of course," said McGurk. "I knew he was the perpetrator almost as soon as we stepped inside his store. The only things I couldn't understand were *how* he made some of those strikes and *why*."

"The means and the motive," I murmured.

"Correct, Officer Rockaway. And the best detective in the world is powerless unless he knows *them*."

The satisfied gleam in his eyes left us in no doubt about which detective he was thinking of.

"Anyway," he went on, "let's take it step—uh—foot-print by footprint. Starting with the afternoon we cleared Whiskers's name . . ."

According to McGurk, it was that incident that put the whole evil idea into Cousin Bob's head.

"I mean, there he was, beavering away, trying to work his way back into his aunt's good graces but getting nowhere very fast. Then—bingo! He saw a surefire way of landing his cousin in deep trouble. After all, Ms. Ennis hadn't been pleased about her niece's cat doing that damage, so what if it could be made to seem that Sandra herself had done something even *worse*? Much worse!"

"Meaning that's when he decided to frame *me*?" said Sandra uneasily.

"Yes. But gradually. Cunningly. One step at a time. . . . So first he selects the largest old boot he can find. Maybe from the dump—"

"Where he probably gets most of his antiques," said Sandra, sniffing.

"And then," said McGurk, "choosing his time, he goes and plants its prints in the Jacobses' pavers. Right next door to Ms. Ennis, where she's bound to get to hear of it."

"And not far from his cousin Sandra's, either," said Wanda, eyeing our client beadily.

"Yes," said McGurk. "But he wasn't ready to frame her just yet. He only wanted to create a sensation at first. To get everyone talking about it and saying what an outrage it was."

"And boy, did he succeed!" said Willie.

"Right," said McGurk. "He even used it to earn himself a few more brownie points with Ms. Ennis by offering to repair her neighbors' pavers for free. And probably that was when he saw the opportunity of doing something that *would* be likely to throw suspicion on his cousin."

"Mrs. Armstrong's goldfish pond?" said our client.

"Yes. Still very sensational, but more a kid's thing."

"But, Chief McGurk," said Mari, "he tried to make it look as if *you* had done that! By using *your* initials—"

"Sure. But only because he knew we were too smart to let *that* pass! He'd seen us in action, remember. With the cats. And he'd realized at the same time—well—" He grinned. "That we and our client weren't exactly close friends. So when we started making out a good case that someone was trying to frame *us*, everyone would soon start to guess who that person was."

"And that's just what we did," said Brains. "Suspect Sandra."

"That's just what *most* of us did," said McGurk. "But don't forget this: Before the U.S.-flag strike, he'd used the boot again. On Mr. Wheeler's concrete strip. Just to make it even more weird and sensational. And in that strike he'd left this behind. . . ."

He reached into the box and pulled out a small plastic bag. It was labeled: SHOTGUN PELLET, FOUND AT SCENE OF CRIME. WHEELER #1.

"Hey, yes!" said Brains. "You still haven't said—"

"Later, Officer Bellingham! What I'm getting at here is that while most of you were thinking that our client had been trying to frame us for the flag prints, *I* couldn't get over the fact that lead shot was found there, too."

This time he pulled out a plastic bag labeled: 2 SHOT-GUN PELLETS FOUND AT THE ARMSTRONG S.O.C.

"And if our client *had* done the Armstrong strike, she must also have made the Hopping Man print at Mr. Wheeler's. And that didn't seem likely at all, being done in the night and probably with a large plank."

Even now Wanda wasn't ready to let Sandra off the hook completely. "But she could have done the Japanese flag. There was no lead pellet at the scene of *that* crime. And it was a deliberate attempt to make Mari and me look guilty!"

Before Sandra could retort, McGurk cut in. "Sure. And he even encouraged our client to come right out and accuse you. By sending the tip-off note. But it was also his first big mistake. He never dreamed we'd trace that note to him in the end—through those Greek *E*s. . . . Anyway, we're getting ahead of ourselves. With the Japanese-flag strike, he knew we'd really be on our toes, targeting his cousin, figuring she had a strong motive for trying to frame us."

"Yeah," growled Wanda. "Like revenge! Spite!"

"And he *also* knew," McGurk continued, "that news of this would soon spread and that it wouldn't be long before Ms. Ennis got to hear."

"So why did he make the paint prints, Chief McGurk?" asked Mari. "On the blacktop and the cars—also the elephant's—when he'd already—?"

"Not so fast, Officer Yoshimura. We're dealing with a criminal genius here. Knowing that sooner or later our client's name would be linked with a general wave of vandalism, he decided to escalate. To make his damage even more outrageous and expensive."

"Including Ms. Ennis's own car," I said.

"Correct. I guess he knew he couldn't expect to be able to frame Sandra for that—"

"But he *tried!*" said Willie. "When we found the elephant's foot and the wolf in his store!"

McGurk shook his head. "That was only because we took him by surprise. He lost his nerve and in his panic he couldn't think of anything better than to try and pin the blame on *her*. I bet he regrets that now. Anyway, using the wolf and the elephant was just to create the maximum shock. And it worked. The wolf prints got your aunt really mad at *all* vandals."

"You can say that again!" muttered Sandra.

"So all that was needed *then* was for us to find the boot he planted in our client's yard and accuse her of some of those earlier strikes." McGurk turned to Sandra.

"Which would have been enough to have your aunt turn against you—right?"

"*More* than enough!" she murmured sadly.

"And sooner or later to chop you from her will— right?"

"Probably sooner!" Sandra said.

"And then put *him* back in it?"

"I guess!" groaned Sandra.

"He'd have made *sure* of it!" said McGurk. "Don't worry—a weasel like him! And he'd have kept his low profile—totally innocent—leaving *us* to do the dirty work of accusing you."

McGurk looked around. "A guy like that, men, I wouldn't put it past him to tell Ms. Ennis how shocked he was. How he just couldn't believe that a nice kid like his cousin could have had anything to do with these things."

"Which would only have made Aunt Jane madder than ever at me!" said Sandra, with tears of indignation in her eyes.

"Exactly!" said McGurk. "A perfect crime. Except for one thing. He made the mistake of trying to use the McGurk Organization for his stooges!"

Then he slapped the table. "And now," he said, "any questions?"

20 Final Questions—and Answers

"Yes, I—"

"One thing still—"

Both Brains and Sandra had spoken at once.

"Our client first, Officer Bellingham," McGurk said politely.

"Huh!" grunted Sandra. "I should think *so*, too!" Then she continued, "One thing still doesn't seem to fit. Why did he send me that note saying the wolf prints had been made with a stencil?"

McGurk nodded. "A good question. . . . Well, I think he'd suddenly had cold feet about the wolf and the damage it caused. Realized he might just have gone over the top with that one and that the police would certainly be called in. I can almost hear him now."

McGurk leaned back, closing his eyes and rocking gently. "I can't imitate his voice like Officer Yoshimura, but here's what he'd be saying. 'Gosh! What if one of the police department's crack detectives is put on the case! *He* might recognize these as real wolf prints. He might even be smart enough to guess they were made by a *stuffed* wolf. He might even be ultrasmart and *persevering* enough to start looking in antiques stores!' "

"But that is—" Mari began.

"So what did cunning old cousin Bob do?" McGurk cut in, opening his eyes. "He thought of the stencil idea—which he'd have been safer doing in the first place. Something even a kid could have done quickly and almost as effectively. And he passed this idea to his cousin Sandra in his note." McGurk grinned. "So of course *she* starts blabbering about it all over the place. Results? One: Hopefully nobody would even think of looking for a real wolf after that, alive or dead. And two: Sandra's measuring and fussing and accusing *us* would only link her name more closely with the damage to her aunt's car." McGurk shook his head. "That cousin of yours! You've got to hand it to him!"

"I—I could *kill* him!" Sandra blurted. Then she blinked. McGurk was staring at her curiously. "Well . . . in a manner of speaking," she muttered.

Mari broke the rather awkward silence. "But Chief McGurk—you were saying how he thought a really *really* smart police-department detective might start suspecting a stuffed wolf. . . ."

"Yes, Officer Yoshimura?"

"Well—that is just what *did* happen. In a way."

"Sure," he said, dipping into the box and producing a plastic bag labeled: HAIR FROM WOLF'S TAIL. FOUND AT DALY S.O.C. "It never crossed the jerk's mind that you don't have to be a member of the police department to be a crack detective. That even a *kid* might qualify. Which is why he was so shocked when *we* visited his store."

Even Sandra was looking at McGurk with respect.

Then Brains piped up. "You *still* haven't said about the lead pellets, McGurk. *Does* he go around carrying a sawed-off shotgun?"

I sat up. Maybe *this* was what had had McGurk talking about murder earlier.

"Okay," he said. "Let's just go back to the first one. Found on the Wheeler strip. And how we ruled out the possibility of our client here making that print."

"Yes," said Brains. "Because it would have meant her carrying a fourteen-foot plank to the scene. And only an adult or an older kid would have the transportation necessary. But—"

"Well, that method—the bridge—might have been good enough for any ordinary adult," said McGurk. "But this guy—well—he *is* a genius."

"So go on, McGurk!" said our client. "How *did* my cousin the genius make that print?"

"In a much neater, quicker way. Yours *was* a good

idea, Officer Yoshimura, but his was better. This!" He removed the boot from the evidence box.

"Well, we *know* he used that," said Wanda. "But how did he get it to the middle without stepping on the wet concrete himself?"

"I'm coming to that," said McGurk, reaching to the floor. He pulled up the broom handle we'd used as a vaulting pole. "He probably had a longer and thicker pole. Like maybe one of those bamboo curtain poles in his store. But all he had to do was push the end of it through these two holes in the boot"—McGurk did this as he spoke—"then stand at the side of the strip and reach out until the boot was over the center. Then lower it onto the wet concrete."

He lowered the boot onto the center of the table.

I was just about to ask if it would be heavy enough to make such a firm impression at that distance when Brains beat me to it. Indirectly.

"But where does the lead shot come in?"

"Let me ask *you* something, Officer Bellingham—as our science expert. What is one of the heaviest substances known?"

"Uh—lead, of course."

"Right. Well, late last night, I was going over the day's events and I happened to remember that old deep-sea diver's helmet in Bob's window and—"

"Hey, yes!" said Brains. "*They* used lead in their boots to—"

"Correct," said McGurk. "And so did he. In this work boot. He filled it with lead shot to give it the weight to make a deep enough impression when he lowered it."

Brains looked as if he could have kicked himself with a lead boot for not thinking of it first. Then he rallied. "Yes, but these holes. They're too close to one end. The center of gravity would be nearer the toe end."

"So?"

"So the boot would tilt forward on its pivot—the pole—with its own weight. It would tend to come down toe end first, not flat."

"Right again, Officer Bellingham. Which is why the print was *deeper* at the toe end, remember? Which was all to the good for Cousin Bob, making it look like a genuine hopping print."

"Gosh, yeah!" murmured Willie.

"And he used lead shot for the smaller shoes, too," McGurk continued. "The Nikes and whatever he made the Japanese flag with. He must have held *them* in his hand. The lead would give them weight, too, so he wouldn't have to waste too much time pressing them in."

"Why not just put an iron bar in?" asked Wanda.

"Using lead shot spread the weight," said McGurk. "Making the impression more even. He probably filled a sock with them first, so that too many loose ones didn't get scattered around. I tell you, that guy's a genius. And he might have gotten away with it, if only he hadn't tried to be *too* smart."

Sandra stood up. "Well, that certainly wraps it up as far as *I'm* concerned. I'll go straight to Aunt Jane now and tell her what we've found out!"

But McGurk advised her against that. "Dumb move!" he said. "*You* keep a low profile. Your aunt's steaming mad about those paint prints, don't forget. You go to her in triumph accusing your cousin, and she might suspect you're getting a kick out of it all, and she won't like *that*, either!"

That pulled Sandra up!

"Well . . . what *are* we going to do? I suppose *you'd* like to be the one to go to her all triumphant!"

"No," said McGurk. "Not to her. To the police. This has been a crime against other people, too. The Jacobses, Mrs. Armstrong, Mr. Wheeler, the Woodstocks, the Dalys, the blacktop crew, and the general public. So right now I aim to take all this evidence to the police and let them handle it from here on in."

A wistful look crossed his face. "After all, *we* can't arrest your cousin. . . . I mean, who knows how dangerous he might be when he realizes he's finally cornered?"

Then he brightened. "And naturally, the police will inform your aunt, so she won't be in any doubt about you being anything more than just another innocent victim. In fact, she might even feel guilty that it was her money that was the cause of it all. I mean—hey!—she might even want to make it up to you with some extra treat or other!"

So that settled that and that's what we did.

For once, the police listened to us patiently. It turned out they'd already had their own suspicions about Cousin Bob as a possible receiver of stolen goods, and all this was icing on the cake for them, giving them probable cause for searching his premises. So, after thanking us and telling us firmly to leave the rest to them, they made a lightning raid that very night.

Too late, though.

Cousin Bob had lit out already. (McGurk thinks that the CLOSED sign had never been turned around since we'd last seen it ourselves.) The guy had taken care to get rid of the wolf and the elephant's foot, of course, but the police found them in the dump the next day.

As for the "criminal genius" himself, he's still on the run. As Patrolman Cassidy told Ms. Ennis, "I don't suppose they'll put the FBI on his trail for a few acts of vandalism, no matter how way-out!"

Sandra reported this when she came to our HQ a few days later and (very grudgingly) told us her aunt wanted to see us sometime soon and thank us personally.

But something else was troubling our client. "You don't *really* think he'd have been violent, do you?"

McGurk shrugged. "Why not? A possible murderer like him?"

"Murderer?" gasped Sandra.

"Sure," said McGurk. "If he'd succeeded, your aunt would have done what he'd hoped and schemed for, wouldn't she? Removed you from the will and put *him* back in it."

"But—you said *murderer,*" faltered Sandra.

"Yes. Because once he'd gotten back, with the chance of inheriting all her money, the lady would still have had to die before he could touch a penny of it. So . . ."

"Gosh—yes!" whispered Sandra.

"A guy like that," said McGurk, "who could plan all those fantastic prints and nearly get someone else blamed—I wouldn't put *anything* past him!"

"Me either!" said Sandra, shuddering.

"Anyway," said McGurk, "thanks to the McGurk Organization, you *didn't* get the blame and that will not happen." He turned to me. "I've been thinking, Officer Rockaway—how about adding this to our notice on the door?"

"This" was a card he'd typed himself:

```
FRAmE-UP FAKERs
     FOILED
```

"Just a minute, McGurk!" Sandra interrupted. " 'Thanks to the McGurk Organization'? Without my input, without *my* detective work, you'd have been nowhere!"

"Oh, no?" he growled.

"No!"

"Well, let me tell you something, Miss Smarty-pants," he said. "All *your* detective work was doing was playing right into his hands!"

"Oh, yeah?"

"Yeah!"

They glared at each other for about thirty seconds. Eyeball to eyeball. Green eyeball to blue eyeball.

Then the blue one blinked, and with that Sandra Ennis flounced out, slamming the door behind her.

Which is why Wanda said, "What did I tell you, McGurk? Sandra Ennis grateful? Don't kid yourself!"

And also why he had me change that notice to:

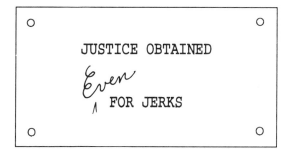